Tribulation

Hilary Lisee

Published by Hilary Lisee, 2024.

TRIBULATION

First edition. June 15, 2024.

Copyright © 2024 Hilary Lisee.

ISBN: 979-8223680109

Written by Hilary Lisee.

To my husband, Jason. Thank you for your love and support through this crazy process!

Chapter 1- After

A tiny bead perched on the tip of her nose, hanging on for dear life before falling to the ground, where it made a small dent in the dry soil on impact. Charlotte tore a small handkerchief from her pocket and wiped the sweat from her face.

The surprising warmth beat down on her from above as she grasped a stubborn weed at the root, pulling it off. Her muscle strained against the seemingly immovable force before it finally relented. Charlotte fell back against the bare ground as a spray of dirt shot into her face, spreading soil into her nose and mouth. She breathed hard, launching several grains on the ground before wiping her mouth with the back of her hand. A triumphant smile plastered her face as she gazed at the stubborn weed in her hand. An enormous crater in the soil mound is the only remnant of her nemesis.

She groaned as she rose and rubbed her sore backside. Charlotte strolled to the large bucket filled to the brim with rainwater. She took the carved ladle off the hook and dipped it into the cool water. The first sip of the sweet water ran down her parched throat, causing a shiver to emerge across her body.

She sighed loudly in relief as she turned to face her latest project. The bare ground loomed before her, with sporadic patches of weeds and tree shoots. The trees behind the garden stood tall. Several pine and fir trees emerged in stark contrast to the oak and maple trees, which had tiny buds on their tips. Charlotte smiled briefly at her land returning to life after the long winter.

"Charwet," a small voice called out from around the corner of the house. The small boy, covered in mud from head to toe, toddled toward her. A chuckle bubbled up inside Charlotte's chest as she stretched her mouth into a neutral face. She placed her hands on her hips before shaking her head.

1

"Paul. What have you got all over you?" A slight grin appeared on her face as the white teeth of his smile shined out behind all the mud.

"Mud, Charwet," he patted his stomach, launching mud across the small space. Several speckles landed on her pants. A loud chuckle forced itself out of her throat as she laughed with abandon. Paul danced before her, spraying mud, his belly laughing echoed against the trees.

As her laughter ceased, she dipped the ladle into the large bucket filled with rainwater and poured it over his head, revealing his sandy blond hair. He giggled as rivulets of mud and water raced across his golden skin. His brown eyes shined beneath his long black lashes.

After several more scoops and the sweep of her handkerchief, Paul's chubby face was clean. Charlotte smiled warmly at the bubbling toddler as he made his way toward the small play area she had set up earlier. Aging metal toy trucks with rust holes Charlotte salvaged from an empty house sat next to an empty mound of dirt. Paul made noises that sounded nothing like an actual dump truck as he pushed them around the area. But Charlotte excused his mistake since he had never heard one before.

Charlotte gazed at the sun and swallowed hard as a few clouds skittered across the sky. In the distance, a bank of dark clouds loomed. She judged that she had about an hour before they would interrupt her daily chores. She returned to her project, pulling the weeds from the garden beds.

She stood as she pulled the final weed from the bed and gazed at the empty soil. It needed some lime before the rain came. As she looked up, a cool wind whipped through her yard, scattering the leaves from last fall. Charlotte shivered as she pulled her shawl tighter across her shoulders and ran to her deteriorating tool shed to grab the lime and a rake. She quickly shook the bag across the beds and mixed it in. That's when she felt it: the first drops of spring rain. Large drops plopped through the dry soil as she raked the final rows quickly.

Hurrying to put her tools away, she spun around to see Paul staring straight into the sky. At that moment, a large drop plopped right into his eyes. He screamed while swatting at his face with his chubby fingers. Charlotte picked him up, and he rubbed his face against her blouse. Then she rushed to the house and shut the door quickly.

As the door closed, the sky opened, letting loose torrents of rain. The rain pelted against the roof with a staccato rhythm. The trees whipped back and forth as the wind rushed through the valley. Charlotte watched in awe as the rain poured down over the land. She prayed that the soil would retain some of the moisture.

Paul lay his head against her shoulder. Tears streaked down his dirty face as he watched the storm with his sister. His small body grew heavy with sleep, and Charlotte swayed lightly to soothe his tired body. She smiled as she felt his breath even out.

She glanced at the rain cleansing the land before she slowly went to their room. She tucked him into his bed and kissed him on his head. Charlotte brushed his bangs out of his face, realizing he needed a haircut. She would add that to her list of chores.

Turning to the wood stove, she stirred the coals and added a few pieces of wood. She blew a small stream of breath over the coal and watched the sticks catch with flames. Closing the door, she placed the kettle on the top of the cast iron surface. She filled the kettle with water before opening jars of preserved vegetables from last season and some dried meats from the market, placed the items into the water and swirled it with her wooden spoons, and then added some dried rosemary and basil before she left the stew to simmer.

She sat down on the rundown couch and grabbed her mending. Paul was growing too fast, and she was constantly fixing his clothing. Once she finished her mending, she needed to warm water for their dishes and maybe a bath later.

She stirred the stew, knowing that Paul would wake soon and be hungry. The savory smell wafted through the kitchen, and her stomach growled. She pressed her hand against it, realizing she hadn't eaten since this morning. *Stupid.* She knew better than to go without food for so long.

She pulled out the last loaf of bread and began slicing it as she felt Paul pressed against her body. His body was still soft with sleep. "Charwet. Hungwee."

She smiled down at him before she patted his head. "Go sit down, Paul. I will bring you some food."

He scurried over to the table and turned to her with a smile as he pulled himself into his seat. She scooped some stew from the pot before placing it carefully in front of him with a couple of pieces of bread.

"Careful Paul. It's hot." He nodded before he reached for the bread and stuffed a large piece into his small mouth.

"Mmmm," he said around the food as he chewed loudly. Charlotte lightly giggled before she grabbed food for herself.

Darkness started to settle around them, so Charlotte lit the lamp in the middle of the table. The shadows skittered around the room, flickering in the flame. The lamp oil was low, and Charlotte mentally noted to get some at the market next weekend. The desolate winter burned more oil than she had expected. She internally cursed herself for not planning better.

Paul finished his meal and rubbed his stomach. "Yum." He rolled carefully from his chair and ran up to Charlotte, saying, "Fank you, Charwet." She curved her arm around his shoulders and pulled him tight against her body, relishing the feel of his little body against hers.

"Grab your plate and bring it to the bucket," she said as she bopped his nose. He giggled and toddled over to his plate. After stoking the fire, she got up and warmed the water. Within minutes, the water was boiling, and she did the dishes of their meager meal. She wrapped the leftover bread and placed the stew into the cold storage. She looked over at Paul and blinked back tears. Chubby hands splashed in the soapy water. His straw-colored hair reminded her of her father. An ever-present ache spread across her chest as she thought of everything she had lost.

Shaking her head, she brought herself back to the present. There was no use dwelling on the things she had lost. It wouldn't change anything.

She made her way over to his side and kissed his head. He splashed once more before looking up at her with dark brown eyes. She smiled down at him, relishing the feeling of contentment sweeping through her soul. While she missed her old life, she would never regret her life with Paul.

"How about a bath?" she said as she finished drying the last plate.

Paul jumped up and down, clapping. She quickly grabbed him before he fell from the stool. "Baff! Baff!" he said as he ran in circles around her legs. Charlotte lightly chuckled before she brought him into the downstairs bathroom. She filled the tub halfway with cold water before pouring in some hot water left on the stove. Paul stripped his clothes as he ran in circles around the tub. She grabbed the honey soap and a washcloth when she finished swirling the water around. Paul jumped in the tub and began playing with his rubber ducks.

"Quack. Quack," Charlotte said as she scrubbed the remaining mud from his hair and body.

Paul picked up one of the ducks and held it to her face. "Wack!" A deep laugh escaped as she rinsed the soap from his hair. She turned to grab the towel before pulling him out of the bath and then rubbed the towel over his head, soaking up most of the moisture before setting him in front of the fire. Dressing him in pajamas, she noticed they were riding up several inches on his leg, and she swallowed hard. She added material onto her mental list for the market that weekend.

As she tried to calculate what she would need to trade for everything she needed, Paul crawled his way up into her lap. His sleepy eyes drifted up to her. "Storwee. Pwease," he requested.

"Of course. What story would you like?" She stroked him gently down the cheek.

He leaned against her chest and said, "Daddy storwee." She froze. Her chest tightened to the point where she thought it would. She managed a shaky breath before looking down at him. She couldn't deny him knowing about their father.

Forcing a smile across her face, she said, "Okay. Daddy story. Let's get in bed." Paul slid down and ran upstairs before he jumped in bed.

She heard the door close downstairs before Jacob's voice drifted to her ears. But she didn't have time to worry about them. She sat slowly on the edge of the bed, her mind fluctuating between calm and panic. She pressed her lips together and closed her eyes. A deep breath infused a momentary calm before she opened them. "Okay, Paul, settle down." He wiggled beneath the covers and laid his head on the pillow. She leaned down to kiss his forehead. "Long ago, before you were born, the world was very different..."

Chapter 2- Before

Charlotte woke the morning it happened with the sun. Daddy was whistling in the kitchen while cooking bacon. The salty smell forced her to get up and stumble into the room. Daddy glanced at her and said, "Good morning, Princess!"

She wrapped her arms around his waist. He placed his arm around her, squeezing her lightly. "Morning, Daddy," she said as she looked up at his cornflower blue eyes, the only part she inherited from him. His pale skin, contrasting to her golden hue, rubbed her shoulder.

"Your mom isn't feeling that good this morning." He patted her shoulder before turning back to the stove. "She couldn't sleep. Paul was moving around a lot last night." He smiled brightly at the mention of her little brother in her mother's tummy. "So, I thought we could make her some breakfast in bed. What do you think?"

Charlotte smiled and said, "Sure, Daddy." She moved the step stool to grab dishes from the cupboard. She placed one on the tray Daddy left on the counter before setting the table with the remaining two. She got out the orange juice and poured three glasses before placing one on the tray.

"Why don't you go out to the garden and pick a few flowers, Princess," he said as he divided the eggs and bacon among the three plates.

Charlotte ran out the door to the garden and picked a few daisies and a multi-colored hollyhock. She placed the flowers into a small vase on the tray before Daddy kissed her on the head. "Thanks, Princess. I'll be right back, and we can eat."

She sat at the table and fidgeted with the napkin before Daddy returned. He brightly smiled as he ruffled her hair, and then they tucked into their meals with minimal conversation. When she finished, she saw Daddy looking at his phone. His face dropped as he stared at the screen. She picked up their plates and took them to the sink.

7

Going to her room to get ready for school, Charlotte heard Daddy's heavy footsteps outside her parent's room. She tiptoed to the doorway and peeked around the corner. She didn't mean to eavesdrop, but she couldn't help but overhear him moving swiftly around the room.

"Glenn. What are you doing?" Mommy asked as she sat up in bed.

"I have been called to New York," Daddy said as he gathered his gear.

"But...But..." Mommy placed her hand on her large belly. Daddy stopped in his tracks. She could almost see the tears in his eyes as he looked over at her large stomach.

He sat on the bed and placed his large hand against her belly. "I know, May. But I have been called to New York. Something has happened. I don't know much, but it must be bad if they call my team in."

Mommy stared at the corner of the room as Daddy dressed in his uniform and got his boots on. Charlotte hadn't seen him in his uniform for a long time. He was so handsome.

Daddy was in the Army Reserves. He had been on active duty until about eight years ago when he decided he needed his family more than the army. But he wasn't ready to give it up completely. So, he stayed in the reserves, knowing he could be called up. Charlotte had heard her parents argue about it more frequently, especially with her little brother on the way. Daddy had promised not to reenlist in his subsequent training in two weeks.

Charlotte ran into her room and threw herself on her bed. Tears spilled over and soaked her pillow. She couldn't believe he was being called up two weeks before he would be done. "Princess?" Daddy stood in the doorway. His uniform solidified the knowledge that he was leaving. Tears continued to stream down her cheeks as she thought about him leaving. "Oh, Princess." He moved swiftly into the room and scooped her body into his arms. She clung to his collar as her body shuddered. He ran his hand down her back as he whispered into her ear. "I'm so sorry."

Charlotte took a shuddery breath as she looked up into his sad eyes. "There is my brave girl." He kissed her forehead. "Now, I know this is a lot to ask of you. But I need you to take care of your mom and brother. Okay?" Charlotte swallowed hard but nodded. "Hopefully, I will be back soon, but if I don't get back before Paul is born. Take care of them. Okay?" She nodded and attempted to put on a brave face. She could do this for her Daddy. "That's my girl." He kissed her head and hugged her in his strong arms. He got up, and Charlotte reluctantly released his body. "I love you, Charlotte."

She swallowed hard before her voice returned. "I love you too, Daddy." He smiled as he left the room for the last time. Charlotte sat there and listened to his heavy footsteps approach the door. She heard the door close, and she jumped. He was gone. Somewhere. And she didn't know when he would return. But he promised to come home, and she knew he would.

Charlotte got up and walked into her parent's room. Her mom sat crying on the bed. "Mommy?" She glanced up and smiled.

"Come here, sweetie." She patted the bed next to her, and Charlotte ran to lie beside her. Charlotte laid her head on her mother's chest and placed her hand on her pregnant belly. Her little brother moved, and she was shocked to see the ripple move across her mother's belly. "He's going to want out soon," she said with a chuckle. "He's running out of room." Charlotte nodded and said, "I guess I should call Helen and put her on standby." Charlotte listened to her mother's steady heartbeat. Her mother's cry shattered the peace around her as she rested in a calm state. "What do you mean she is gone, David? Helen would never leave you." She was silent for a few moments. "She disappeared? But that makes no sense! David?" Her body went rigid as Charlotte moved to her Daddy's spot on the bed. She took a deep breath of his musky scent. "Okay. Okay. I'll see you in a few minutes," she said before hanging up the phone. "Charlotte. We need to get dressed. David and Jacob are on their way over."

Charlotte smiled at the thought of her best friend, Jacob. She jumped off the bed and ran to her bedroom. Throwing on some clothes, she realized that it was a school day. "Mommy?" She skidded into her mother's room. "What about school?"

Her mother smiled, but it didn't reach her eyes. "Don't worry about school today, sweetie. It was canceled." Charlotte smiled widely before running back to her room to put on her shoes. She couldn't wait to see Jacob. She looked out her window at the treehouse, their spot.

Charlotte and Jacob had gone to school together before. He was annoying then, but she warmed up when he defended her against some older kids who had pushed her in the dirt at recess. Despite being half their size, he stood up to them, and she was grateful.

So many things were running through her mind that she didn't realize how much time had passed. The door opened, and she heard voices. She immediately skidded into the living room and froze upon seeing Jacob and David standing in the doorway. Jacob clung to his father's hand. His face streaked with tears. Eyes wide, he blinked rapidly when his father pushed him in her direction. Charlotte tried to smile as Jacob slowly made his way across the room. She grabbed his hand and pulled him out to the treehouse.

Jacob slowly ascended the rungs and plopped onto the beanbag in the corner. Charlotte sat in the other beanbag, keeping Jacob at the side of her peripheral. His eyes focused on the floorboard. After several minutes, Jacob said, "My mom is gone." Just like that. Blank. No emotion. As Jacob kept talking, Charlotte blinked rapidly, desperate to find some words. "She just disappeared this morning. No word. No note. Nothing. Just gone." He swallowed hard. "The only thing left was her nightgown."

Charlotte grabbed his hand and said, "There must be a reason. Did she take any of her stuff? Her purse or her phone?"

"No," he said as he got up and walked to the window. Charlotte followed. "Her purse was on the counter, and her phone was plugged in." David raked his hand through his hair. "It doesn't make any sense!"

"Did your dad call the police? Maybe somebody took her?"

"Yeah." He picked at the wood on the sill. "The police didn't pick up at first. But my dad kept trying, and the person said they would add it to the list."

List? Charlotte followed Jacob up into the tree house. "Did the police say anything else?" Jacob shook his head in disagreement. Charlotte grabbed his hand, hoping it would be enough to show him she was there. But he just stared out the window.

"My dad left today." Jacob's head snapped up. "He was recalled to New York or something."

Jacob squeezed her hand. "Something bad is going on. My dad didn't say anything, but I can tell," Charlotte nodded as she spoke. They were silent for several moments. Thoughts swirled through Charlotte's head. *There was a list. A list of missing people. Were they dead or alive?* Charlotte didn't know. "I think there are more people." Jacob broke the silence.

"More people?" she said, her heart pounding. Did she really want to know?

Jacob nodded and said, "More missing people."

Charlotte's eyes widened. Her brain couldn't wrap around the thought that other people were missing. It didn't seem possible. She patted his hand and said, "I'm sure we'll find out."

Jacob nodded, but it didn't seem like he believed it. Charlotte didn't know if she believed it either.

"Jacob!" David called out the back door. "Time to go!"

Jacob got up and dusted off his pants. "Coming, Dad!" He turned and pulled Charlotte in for a hug. She relished the comfort of her best friend. They embraced for several moments before he stepped back.

A chill went through her body as he released her. She pushed her toe through the leaves as Jacob descended the ladder.

Charlotte sat, trying to think over everything that had happened that morning. But her head began to ache like a vise, squeezing tighter with each thought. She made her way down the ladder and into the house. Her mother had the television on.

"A 747-airplane crashed in rural Missouri today. Two hundred seventy-five people are presumed dead. Authorities on the scene found the bodies of around 200 people. The pilots were not among the recovered bodies. In other news, President Wallace, Vice President Yarris, and several key cabinet members have also disappeared. Several witnesses stated that people were there one minute and gone the next. Authorities are struggling to keep up. At the latest, over 150 million people are gone. No one knows why they disappeared, but reports are slowly trickling in."

150 million people? What was happening? Charlotte gasped, and her mother jumped. "Oh, sweetie. I am so sorry." She turned off the television. Charlotte wanted to protest but didn't want to upset her mom. "You shouldn't have seen that," said her mom.

"What is happening, Mommy?" Charlotte rushed to her mother's side and climbed on her lap. Her mom wrapped her arms around her and snuggled her as best as possible around her protruding stomach.

Her mother sighed and said, "I don't know, sweetie. No one does."

Chapter 3- After

"Daddy left to defend our country when the worst happened. He is out there somewhere and will return to us when he's done," Charlotte said as she stroked her finger down Paul's cheek.

She tried to keep the doubt from her voice. Four years. No contact. He was probably dead. In her mind, she knew this was most likely true. However, she didn't want to admit it completely. That would mean they were all alone.

His eyes fluttered open briefly. "Daddy, hewo."

"That's right. Daddy's a hero." She smiled as he took a shuddery breath and closed his eyes. His body softened with sleep, and Charlotte rubbed his back as his breaths evened. He always went to sleep quickly, even as a baby.

Charlotte drained the water from the tub before refilling it with hot water. She shucked her clothes and placed them in the bin. A loud sigh escaped her mouth as she sank into the heat. It soothed her sore muscles, unused to the torture of the day.

It was always this way in the spring when her body came out of hibernation—especially this winter when the long nights and short days were filled with little entertainment and chores.

She quickly washed her body as the water began to cool in the evening air. Despite the wood-burning stove, their rooms were chilly and often damp.

Charlotte mentally added the repair to her ever-growing list of chores as she pulled herself out of the tub. Water dripped onto the rag rug as she quickly dried and dressed in flannel pajamas she made from her father's shirt. The soft fabric hugged her body like a fluffy blanket and soothed her heart. A piece of her father surrounded her every move.

She drained the tub again, rolled it into the spare room, and then went to the stove. A blast of heat reached out and swirled around her like a flying dragon. She banked the fire, relishing the warmth from the open door that chased away the chill.

Charlotte checked on Paul. His quilt laid askance from his frequent movement. He was sideways across the bed, but she knew it wouldn't be long before he moved again. She pulled the quilt around him as best as possible before retreating to the bed in the other corner.

Pulling her quilt around her legs, she reached for her list, making several entries for future chores. Looking over at Paul, she realized it was time to begin teaching him the act of survival. She noted several chores Paul could help with and closed her book.

A shiver wound down her spine as she pulled the blanket firmly over her shoulders. She grabbed the radio that sat just beyond her head. A high-pitched whine accompanied the winding of the charging lever before she placed it on the small table. She turned the dial, allowing light static to fill the silent room. Charlotte turned the tuner knob, and a droning voice cut through the static.

A bomb went off today in the capital. Multiple buildings were destroyed, and more than 300 people were killed. America Strong claimed responsibility for the attack. The Collective requested military assistance in tracking down the individuals responsible.

Fighting broke out on the border of Massachusetts and New Hampshire over food shortages at the government-managed facilities, forcing hundreds of families to find alternative food sources. The military subdued the fighting quickly despite several injuries without a single loss of life.

The current total number of people who have disappeared stands at 4,358,453,054. While The Collective has determined that the original disappearances were due to an unexplained phenomenon, they are still looking into more recent disappearances that have been reported. The Collective will continue updating the public as more information becomes available.

Charlotte twisted the dial off as static returns. The same message would repeat in a few minutes. She scooted deeper into the bed and pulled her quilt tighter around her body to ward off the chill. She couldn't believe the number of disappearances across the world.

Her mind drifted to the fighting in New Hampshire. Food scarcity was familiar, especially in her area. The government established regional food distribution in the larger metropolitan areas two years ago. Charlotte heard about them on the radio with no chance of ever seeing one.

Her mind drifted to the mention of the military. Four years was way too long for her father to be gone. A small part of her hoped she would see him again.

She folded her hands underneath her face as she thought about him. Would he be proud of her? She hoped so. Charlotte had protected her family despite being ill-equipped for the task.

Her gaze flicked to Paul sprawled across the mattress. A small smile crossed her face as she took in her greatest accomplishment. He was alive because of her. Their life was not glamorous, but it was life. And she would protect it with everything she had.

Chapter 4- After

It was market day. After the first winter, Charlotte realized she would need a way to get things. She began curing meats that Jacob and David hunted in the woods. Her jerky was raved about at the market.

She moved into the room and observed Paul sitting quietly on the floor. Action figures and blocks were spread around him. Charlotte moved toward him as he smiled at her. He offered her one of the action figures, and she sat beside him. "Not today, Paul." A deep frown lodged on his chubby face. "Don't look at me like that, Paul. You know it is market day." She moved toward him and began tickling his belly. A large snort followed by deep belly laughs echoed through the enclosed space.

"Stop...Charwet." He wiggled against the quilt before he got up and ran for their little bathroom. Paul careened back to the floor and plopped in the middle of his toys. She ran her hand down his head, and he wiggled out of reach.

She stood and gave him a small smile, then exited the room and made her way down the stairs. David sat at the kitchen table eating some toast. "Paul upstairs?"

"Yeah, he's a little disappointed," she said as she moved to the pantry. She gathered her extra jars of jerky and dried items she made for the market.

As she returned to the kitchen, David said, "We'll find something fun to do." He finished eating and took his plate to the sink.

She grabbed her market items and walked to the door, then she shut the door and took a deep breath. Her heart beat heavily as she wrapped her shoulder bags across her neck.

Her foot sank slightly into the soggy, spongy wood steps. Moss grew in clumps around the railings of the old wheelchair ramp. The newer steps were one misstep away from collapse. They would need to be reinforced this summer.

Patches of ice clung to the shadowy forest beyond her home, betraying the spring warmth. Streaks of sunlight punctuated from the clouds scattered through the blue sky. The heat warmed her. Charlie slipped her father's sunglasses over her eyes as she trekked down the driveway. Her feet crunched against the gravel. Charlie hopped along, dodging the large potholes filled with icy water. She inhaled deeply, taking in the acrid smell of woodsmoke in the distance—a familiar and welcome scent.

She skirted closer to the tree line as she approached the road. Her eyes scanned the area for any movement. While The Watchers were uncommon in the area, they popped up occasionally. Based on gossip, they were looking for children without parents. Children like me. Silence permeated the air, and she let out the breath she hadn't realized she was holding.

A whistle sounded from her right, and she jumped instantly on edge. Her heart beat staccato in her chest as she frantically searched for origin. She kicked the dirt hard and scowled when she noticed Jacob bent in half laughing.

"You nearly scared me to death!" The tension in her chest released as she strolled across the road toward her friend.

He continued to chuckle as he made his way to her. "Well, you would have heard me coming if you were paying attention. I called your name about ten times before I whistled," Jacob said. He ran his hand through his hair, and she shivered lightly.

Heat suffused her cheeks as she looked at her feet. Her father had warned her of the danger of a wandering mind. Yet, for some reason, she couldn't help herself. She had too much to think about.

"Really?" She kicked her feet through the dirt. Small clouds of dust twirled with the wind as it blew gently away.

Jacob touched Charlotte's shoulder and said, "Don't feel bad. I get like that, too." Charlotte managed a small smile while internally berating herself for her lack of focus. She knew dangers lurked in the darkness. "Are you ready for the market?"

She nodded and began walking down the road. Jacob caught up and paced himself. Her feet took twice as many steps as his longer legs. Silence punctuated by their footsteps on the pavement enveloped their walk back up the next hill.

Lost in thought, Charlotte stumbled over a piece of road that must have pushed up over the winter. Her body pitched forward, and her heart stuttered as she watched the jagged edge nearing her leg. Jacob stopped her freefall and lifted her away. Her feet dangled off the pavement for a moment before he set her down. Her legs wobbled but firmed with his arms around her.

"Jeez, Charlotte," Jacob said as he wiped his brow. "What's up with you today?"

Her face heated with embarrassment. She shrugged and kept walking. Tears pricked the corner of her eyes as she thought about his words. She swallowed hard but forced her eyes to follow the road. His arm pulled her to a stop, and she avoided eye contact until he pulled her chin to face him.

"What is it?" his voice was stern. Charlotte finally met his eyes, which softened. "Aww. Charlotte." His arms wrapped around her as he pulled her in for a hug. Rivulets of water ran down her face and pooled on his shirt from embarrassment and sheer exhaustion.

As her tears dried, Jacob pulled back and ushered her to a rock on the side of the road. He handed her a canteen with fresh water. Charlotte gave him a small smile as she took a long swallow. The sweet water trickled down her throat and soothed the ache.

Jacob kneeled in front of her and said, "Feeling better?" She nodded, still unable to voice the fears in her heart. He grimaced, almost like he could tell she wouldn't talk. "Okay, Charlotte. We don't have to talk about it." She sighed internally, relieved her fears were safe for another day. She moved to stand up, but Jacob stepped just in front of her and assured, "But just know. If you need to talk, I am here."

"I know, Jacob," she said. He nodded and stepped away. They both walked to the top of the hill immediately preceding the market. Jacob pulled out his binoculars at the overlook and peered down at the school in the distance.

"It looks clear." While typically safe, the market was still illegal in the new government. The local leaders would fly a United States flag upside down to keep everyone safe if there was trouble.

Jacob handed Charlotte the binoculars. Charlotte focused on the market and scanned the area. People were milling around the various stands. A few children scooted between the legs of the adults. When she moved to the flagpole, the town flag, yellow with a large bear in the middle, flew at half-mast.

"Yeah, it looks good," Charlotte said, handing the binoculars back to Jacob before slinging her pack across her chest.

They strode down the road, side by side, as it flattened and curved until the old school came into view. Vines weaved over the exterior of the brick building, concealing broken windows and large glass doors that had fallen off their hinges. The community had fixed the gym roof last summer to hold the market over the winter; otherwise, the building was a shadow of its former glory—the true pillar of the small community.

Food stands littered the parking lot, and people circulated through them. It seemed like more people were there than usual. Charlotte adjusted her backpack before they walked up to the credit table. Jacob went first and handed over a couple of whittled sculptures, two wooden spoons, and a few jars of dried fruit from their orchard. Mr. Jordan, the market leader, smiled at his offerings and gave him his credits.

Charlotte pulled out her jerky jars and the hide blanket she had made from the deer she hunted last Fall. Mr. Jordan's eyes lit up as he examined the blanket. He nodded before he handed her two twenty-dollar chips and a five-dollar chip. Her eyes widened in surprise. "Thank you," she whispered as she stared at the tokens in her hand. A small smile stretched across his face as he nodded and placed the items into a wheelbarrow behind him.

Charlotte turned into the market area, still overwhelmed by the large amount of chips in her pocket. That would buy Paul a few outfits and possibly a new pair of shoes. It might even treat her to some of her favorite honey soap. She headed straight for Mrs. Jordan's clothing stall.

Racks of neutral browns and reds punctuated with sporadic pink or purple surrounded the largest stall in the center of the market. Mrs. Jordan, the purveyor, perched on a stool underneath a slightly collapsed umbrella. A fan flicked in her hand as she watched the shoppers around her stall.

Charlotte dove into the middle of the racks, searching for a couple of pairs of jeans for Paul. His current clothes were about two inches too short. She pulled a pair of linen pants with a jagged hem and jeans with patches over the knees. Charlotte sighed as she looked over the state of the clothing.

She grabbed a couple of T-shirts and made her way to Mrs. Jordan. "Mornin'," Charlotte said as she placed the items on the makeshift counter.

"Mornin' Charlotte." Mrs. Jordan looked over the clothing and grimaced. "Sorry about the state of things. Not as easy to get clothes these days." She took the hangers and placed them in a basket at her feet. Gently folding them, she offered them to Charlotte. "That'll be 15 credits."

Charlotte's eyes widened at the price. "A... a...are you sure?" she stuttered as she looked between the pile of clothes and Mrs. Jordan.

Mrs. Jordan smiled and placed the clothes in Charlotte's hands. "Of course, dear. They are not up to my normal standard." Charlotte fished a twenty-dollar credit from her pocket. Mrs. Jordan smiled as she handed back a slip with a five-dollar credit. "Have a wonderful day, Charlotte. Say hi to Paul for me," she said.

Charlotte nodded as she quickly stuffed the clothes into her bag and stepped away from the booth. She quickly scanned the lot and headed toward the apiary stand. "Mornin' Charlotte!" Mr. Jacobs boomed as she approached.

She waved as she made her way to the honey soap. The scent of lavender and honey surrounded her as she inhaled its fragrance. Her mind wandered to the harvest festival last spring. Fields of purple as far as the eye could see. Good food. "Perfect choice," Mr. Jacobs said.

She smiled and asked, "When is the harvest festival?"

"Next weekend!" Mr. Jacobs responded. He rattled on about the events he had planned for the harvest festival. The lavender harvest was the main event but also hayrides and a mud pie contest. Paul particularly loved that one. The food was excellent, and all were provided free of charge for help with the harvest. Honey-covered biscuits were Charlotte and Paul's favorites. "Is your family going?"

"Gotta check with David, but I think so," Charlotte said as she handed him her five-dollar credit, internally cringing at the high price. But it was worth it. His product was legendary.

"Have a great day, Charlotte!" Mr. Jacobs said as he turned to help another customer.

Charlotte waved as she headed into the crowd in search of Jacob. Her eyes scanned the parking lot as a loud siren wailed through the dusty space. The Watchers were coming. People hurried through the parking lot. Children screamed as parents scooped them up.

A man slammed into Charlotte, causing her to tumble onto the broken pavement. His black eyes bore into her with a leering smirk plastered on his face. Rotten breath skittered across her skin as his hand crept toward her. Charlotte scuttled backward like a crab and jumped as the man was tackled. Jacob's unruly mop bounced around his head as he pressed the man to the ground. The man held his hands up in surrender, peering at Charlotte one last time. Jacob cocked his arm back as the man got up from the ground and ran straight for the woods behind the school.

Fear froze her vision as she watched him run. Jacob's hand thrust into her vision as the last vestiges of the man disappeared into the woods. "We've got to go, Charlotte."

She nodded as she placed her shaking hand into his. He pulled her to her feet, and she brushed her hands over the scrapes on her palms, wincing with each movement. With her hand grasped tightly, Jacob ran for the woods at the side of the market. He jumped over the fence and carefully pulled her over beside him. After her feet hit the ground, he took off running for the tree line as the rumble of trucks crested the hill above.

She crashed through the trees and into the swamp that surrounded the market. Her feet sunk into the foul ooze that seeped into her boots. She cried out as her feet locked in the sucking mud.

Jacob turned back and grabbed her as the Watchers rumbled into view. Large military trucks trundled over the bumpy road. Machine guns were mounted on the top, with at least five heavily armed men surveying the area. Jacob scurried into the woods closer to the school with Charlotte thrown over his shoulder. She watched silently as the men grew more alert as they approached the now-empty lot.

Bare trees and fallen logs were their only protection from the army knocking on their door. Jacob and Charlotte lay behind a large fallen log among the decaying leaves. Her breaths ragged as she attempted to calm her racing heart. She prayed that everyone made it to safety.

Jacob peered over the log with his binoculars as the trucks rolled to a stop in the parking lot. Multiple men disembarked and fanned out across the lot. The sound of cocking rifles echoed through the space. A large man jumped off the back of the truck. "Search everywhere!" he commanded as he scanned the area.

Jacob slowly slid the binoculars over to her. She peered through the lenses and watched the commander stoop and retrieve something from the ground. A pink plastic bracelet hung from his finger. He gazed at the cheap trinket for several seconds before a wide smile slinked across his face. "They're here, boys!" he shouted. "Let's get 'em."

Charlotte froze. Her hands clung to the binoculars. Jacob lay down behind the log and began digging. His hands slowly removed the earth from our side of the log. Keeping an eye on the men, she watched as they checked the doors and promptly broke them down. The men poured into the school like bees swarming a hive.

Jacob's head popped up like a meerkat as a woman screamed in the distance. We watched as a woman and a child we didn't know were brought out. "We didn't do anything! Let me go!" Her voice quivered as she searched. "What are you doing with my baby? Where is she?"

Charlotte watched with rapt attention as the woman's hands were bound and a gag strung through her mouth. Her muffled screams could still be heard in the silent forest. Jacob slunk back down and continued digging.

No matter what was happening beneath her, Charlotte couldn't take her eyes off the mother. The commander pushed her to her knees as the soldier swept the crying child away to one of the vehicles. Tears streamed down the mother's face as she watched her child disappear. Gut-wrenching sobs escaped her mouth as she begged for her daughter.

"This woman is unclean! She is tainted!" the commander shouted. His pistol hung loosely at his waist. Charlotte's chest tightened as he continued his speech. "For crimes against the Collective! For belief in a false prophet!" The man ripped a necklace off her neck and threw it to the ground. "The Watchers take custody of the child! And sentence this woman to death!" He lifted his pistol and pulled the trigger. Charlotte pulled back. Tears streamed down her face as she listened to the gunshot echo throughout the valley. "Let this be a lesson to all the unclean out there! We are watching!"

Frozen against the ground, Charlotte shook with fury and deep sadness. Her body trembled. Her heart fought with her mind about whether to rescue the daughter. She moved to peek at the scene until Jacob grabbed her arm. He silently begged her to stay put, and she sighed. He motioned for her to join him under the log, and she quickly moved into the small space. Jacob's larger frame curled around her. His large arms pulled her tight against her as he moved leaves to cover their hideout.

"What was that?" a voice said on the other side of the log. A foot crunched above them, and Charlotte's breath seized inside her. Dirt and bark tumbled around them as several other feet trundled over the log. With each step, Jacob tightened his grip. His breath escaped in small gasps against her neck, causing tingles to spread across her body.

The footsteps encountered the swamp. "Look! Footprints!" Charlotte inhaled quickly. They had found where she had gotten stuck in the mud; it was only a matter of time. The wall closed around her as panic began steadily descending into her system. Jacob's fingers rubbed against her wrist, pulling her away from the fog that threatened to consume her. She nodded briefly to indicate she had returned.

Boots thumped against the ground around them as they returned to the parking lot. "Footprints, sir. Two sets. Looks like they escaped into the woods to the East."

"Thank you, soldier." The vehicles started up. "Time to load up boys!" Feet pounded against the pavement in an asynchronous rhythm. "To anyone that can hear us! Don't forget! We are watching!" His cackling laugh echoed as the door closed, and the vehicles rumbled out of the parking lot, slowly getting quieter and quieter as the distance increased.

Finally, silence rained around Charlotte. She wiggled for a moment, but Jacob still held her firm. "Wait." His breathy whisper caused another chill to run down her spine.

A cicadae's song broke several minutes of tense silence in the afternoon heat. Charlotte sighed as Jacob loosened his grip on her body. She scrambled to escape the small space and create some distance between them. She brushed the remaining dirt from her pants, wincing as her boot squished with every step. As if remembering the moments before she hid, Charlotte faced the school. A small group of people were laying a quilt over the body. Her body trembled as she took a cautious step in that direction.

Jacob crawled out and pulled her into a fierce hug. An overwhelming feeling of both safety and repulsion swept through her body. Each was battling the other. Her arms hung limp at her sides.

The woman's eyes made contact for a moment before tears streamed down her cheeks as she begged. The image flipped through her mind like a movie clip on repeat. The loud bang echoed through her mind every time she closed her eyes.

Shaking her head to remove the images, she stepped away from Jacob. His arms slid across her shoulder. His eyes looked down as he clenched his fists. Charlotte swallowed hard to remove the strangling lump in her throat.

Jacob took a deep breath and patted her lightly on the shoulder. Her body seized from the contact. She didn't want to feel better. A woman died today. The Watchers took her daughter. She fingered the small cross nestled against her throat. That could have been her.

Her body shook with restrained fury. She wanted to scream. To cry. But she couldn't. It wouldn't solve anything. It wouldn't bring the woman back to life. She settled for strolling toward the crowd gathered around the body. Amazing Grace surrounded the survivors in the parking lot as the sun lowered in the sky.

Chapter 5- Before

The phone rang, and Mommy rushed to pick it up. "Glenn, what is going on? Helen is gone. I don't know..."

Daddy's gruff voice stopped my mother. "Put me on speaker." Mommy put the phone down. "Charlotte, are you there?"

"Yes, Daddy." Charlotte gripped her mother's skirt.

Daddy sighed. "I don't know how long I can talk. Things are bad out here. The president is missing. Several cabinet members. Everything is crazy." He paused when a voice spoke in the background. "I'll be right there, Captain. Charlotte, I need you to clean out the safe room in the basement. We live far enough out of town that this shouldn't affect you too much, but I need you and maybe Jacob or David to board up the windows on the house. Get the safe room ready in case you need it." Daddy paused. "There should be at least a year's worth of MREs and water treatment tablets. I need you to tend the garden and preserve as much food as possible. I don't know how long, but we won't have electricity soon. The phones won't last long, either. Tell David...Alpha..."

"Daddy!" Charlotte yelled.

His voice warbled on the other end like he was losing the signal. "Love you...both...Safe." The phone cut out and went silent. Mommy pressed the button several times, but the dial tone was gone.

Mommy sat there. Empty eyes stared into the distance. "Mommy. Mommy!" She shook her head.

"Charlotte. Can you run down to Jacob's and see if they can help us?" Charlotte nodded and skidded out the door. She ran down the long dirt road onto the main street. Empty cars littered the sides of the road. Most of them wrapped around trees or in the ditches. Charlotte ran down the familiar road; her breath came out in puffs as she forced herself to keep moving. Jacob was feeding the horses when she ran into the driveway.

He dropped the bucket and ran for her. "Charlotte, what's wrong?" David stepped out of the barn. Charlotte heaved in deep breaths, attempting to calm her racing heart. "Get her some water, Son," David said as he led Charlotte to the porch swing.

After several minutes, she had gathered enough breath. "Mommy...sent me..." She took several deep breaths. "Heard from Daddy."

Tears perched on the edge of her eyes, threatening to spill over the edge. "It's bad. He said something about Alpha?"

David nodded. "Son. Get the tools into the truck. Glenn told me that if anything happened, I should follow the emergency protocol." David got up and ran to the barn to collect some items. Charlotte sat bewildered by everything around her. The world spun and went in and out of focus. "Charlotte, honey. Let's get you home to your mama. Okay?" Charlotte nodded and wobbled as she stood up. "Jacob!" Jacob came running around the corner. "Help Charlotte into the truck." Jacob took one look at Charlotte and came running. She rapidly blinked as he wrapped a blanket around her. "She's in shock, Son. Just pick her up, and let's go."

"Jacob?" Charlotte croaked as he lifted her off the ground.

Jacob smiled down at her. "It's okay, Charlotte. We'll get you home."

She rested her head against his chest and closed her eyes, slipping into darkness.

"What's wrong with her?" Mommy said as she opened the door.

David walked inside. "She's in shock, May." Mommy gasped. "It's okay. She's going to be okay. Let's get her into her bed."

Jacob walked her into her room and gently laid her on the bed. "There you are, Charlotte. Get some rest. Dad and I will get everything ready." He tucked her in and smiled. Charlotte couldn't remember if she smiled back, but she blissfully found sleep moments later.

The sun was down when she woke to loud hammering noises. Mommy was sitting on the edge of the bed, carefully stroking her hair. "Welcome back, sweetie."

"What happened? What's that noise? What..."

"Shhh..." Mommy pulled her into her arms and rubbed slow circles around her back. "It's okay, sweetie. David and Jacob put boards up on the windows, and they cleaned out the safe room. Hopefully, we don't have to use it..." Her mother trailed off as her hand stilled on Charlotte's back.

Charlotte glanced at the doorway. David filled the doorway. "It's done, May. The windows are boarded. The oil lamps are scattered throughout the house. We pulled some vegetables from the garden and used the meat in the fridge. Moved all the other meat and veggies to cold storage downstairs. Glenn was prepared for this type of thing."

Mommy nodded. "Thank you so much, David. We couldn't have..."

"Nonsense, May," David said. "You are family. If you ever want to come..."

Mommy shook her head. "No. But thank you. I think we will be fine here."

"Okay. Well, we need to get going. But we'll check on you in a few days...maybe a week?"

Mommy stood and hugged David. Jacob stood in the background and gave Charlotte a small wave. Charlotte waved back, wishing her best friend hadn't seen her this way. She curled around her stuffed bear—the one her father won at the Blue Hill Fair. She closed her eyes and prayed for this nightmare to be over.

Chapter 6- After

Charlotte's footstep squished against the moss gathered on the front porch of their ranch house. She paused, listening for any signs of danger. A cool breeze caused shivers to break across her body as the last vestiges of the sun dipped below the horizon.

Jacob hovered behind her. She carefully pulled the door open and stepped inside. Her shoes squished with mud against the wood floors, but she removed them before entering the kitchen. Her body drained of energy as she lifted the latch allowing light to spill into the dark room. The scent of stew wafted through the opening, making her mouth salivate. It was David's venison stew.

David's head peered around the corner of the room. Paul's tinny laughter echoed through the space, and Charlotte smiled despite the guilt, dread, and remorse swirling in her gut.

"Charwet!" Paul popped up from beside David as he rushed toward her. He jumped into her arms, forcing her to sit on the floor, and wrapped his entire body around her. "I missed yew."

Holding him tight against her, she relished the warmth his tiny body gave to her body and heart. He was safe. The extraneous fear sloughed off her as she inhaled his little boy's scent. A combination of fresh grass, wood smoke, and soap from last night's bath trickled into her nose and assured her mind that he was real. "I missed you too, Paul." Her voice was soft against his fierce hug.

Footsteps echoed across the floor, and she froze. Her arms swung Paul behind her as her brain registered the gait. Jacob.

Deep, heaving breaths escaped her as she released Paul before tremors skittered across her body. David's eyes changed momentarily as he grabbed the quilt from the back of the couch and approached Charlotte. "Small breaths, girl." His deep voice soothed her frayed nerves as large arms encircled her trembling form. The quilt formed around her shoulders while Charlotte focused on her breaths.

While she didn't have attacks very often anymore, it usually took a while to diminish when she did have one. A warm, firm hand gripped hers, but her blurry eyes wouldn't reveal the owner. Warbly voices surrounded her. She kept trying to turn her head to locate the speaker but couldn't figure out the correct direction. Her head flopped like a fish as she attempted to ascertain the garbled sound through the whooshing pulse in her ears.

Minutes or maybe hours passed, and she couldn't keep track of time in her incapacitated state before a small voice pierced her mind.

"Charwet?" Paul's voice seemed far away, but she tumbled back into reality when his small hand touched her cheek.

Her vision cleared before her ears. The warbling swirl of voices continued their endless chatter as she stared into the chocolate orbs before her. A tinkling laugh accompanied small fingers squishing her cheeks until her lips puckered. Paul smacked a kiss on her lips and pulled a heavy chuckle that quickly became rolling laughter. She pulled Paul onto her lap as her senses returned to normal; his small arms encircled her neck.

Paul's pajamas scratched against her skin. A stray tear leaked from her eye as she realized how long she had been trapped. Ignoring the prickling stares of David and Jacob, Charlotte picked Paul up and made her way up the stairs to their room. She brushed his bangs from his eyes and kissed him all over his chubby cheeks as she tucked him into bed. Deep belly laughs echoed through the space, quickly replaced with a gaping yawn. Paul's eyes drooped. "I wuv yew, Charwet."

Her heart soared as she whispered, "I love you too, baby." Within moments, Paul was asleep. She tucked the quilt around him, taking a few more moments before facing the two people downstairs.

She steeled her nerves as she walked back down the stairs and met two almost identical faces. The only difference was the bushy beard with patches of gray on David's face.

Charlotte didn't want to admit that the day's events had affected her. She swallowed hard as she stared at the two men in her kitchen. Seconds later, she flinched as the image of the woman collapsing against the pavement skittered across her mind. She closed her eyes to stem the tears pricking at her eyes.

"Charlotte." Jacob's deep voice pulled her from the memory. His chocolate eyes bored into hers like hardened Hershey's Kisses, but they softened as he approached me. He cupped her face and said, "Don't go back there." He kissed her forehead, and a shiver skittered down her spine, tingling through her body to her toes. She swallowed hard and nodded before turning to busy herself in the kitchen.

As she wiped the counters for the third time, David touched her shoulder, and she paused. "Come sit down and eat, girl." Charlotte turned and made her way to the small table while fisting her hand to expel the tremors that continued to plague her since this afternoon.

She didn't know why this had affected her so much. In the last four years, she had endured so much that she was spilling over, but watching that woman… No, she wouldn't go there.

She took a deep breath as she sat on the bench. The aroma of venison stew wafted into her nostrils, and her stomach growled loudly. She giggled lightly before looking up at David and Jacob, staring intently. Their lips were fixed in matching grins.

"Thank you," she said, her voice barely a whisper as she took a large spoonful of the stew. The hearty broth mixed with carrots, potatoes, and venison soothed her frazzled nerves and settled heavily in her stomach.

All too soon, her bowl was empty. "You want more, girl?" David asked. She shook her head as he cleared the bowl from the table and quickly washed it before stacking it on the shelf. Jacob was packing the leftover stew before storing it in the cold room.

David sat heavily on the other bench, perched his fingers against his lips. She swallowed hard. His grin from earlier was missing. "Charlotte. Talk to me, girl. Jacob filled me in on the events, but it has affected you."

Her chest seized while continuing to beat hard in her chest. "What's there to say? She's dead. Like so many others." The last words were barely a whisper.

David's eyes closed for a moment. A whisper of emotion passed over his face, but it was quickly erased as he opened his eyes. "Girl." His voice growled low as Charlotte's eyes widened. David was usually easygoing going, but he was fiercely protective. "Don't lie to me."

Charlotte had learned early on to stand up for herself. "What! It's the truth! She is dead. Not coming back." Tears began to leak down Charlotte's cheeks. Her legs buckled. "She's not coming back." Her voice was barely a whisper, drowned out by the moans and sobs that escaped her body. Her body quaked as she released the demon that constantly rode just below the surface. The soul-sucking pain that she swallowed down deep each day to survive.

A large pair of arms encircled her spare body and pressed her in a body-crunching hug, leaving her lungs with little chance to inflate. However, it was nothing compared to the heaviness that had settled around her soul, crushing it with each passing day. Survival. That was her mission.

She squirmed against the oppressive heat, almost like she didn't deserve anything more before the silent tears streamed down her cheeks. Hands caressed her back as her eyes poured her despair onto his shirt and the floor.

David's growly voice echoed in the small space as the invasion lessened, allowing her to take a deep breath. "Girl. You are stronger than you think." Charlotte shook her head fiercely like a little kid throwing a temper tantrum. She was weak. Her wet face proved that. "Look at me," David said.

Her eyes widened as she met the determined orbs above her. "Think about that boy upstairs." David's hand grasped her shoulder, and she looked back into his eyes. "That boy is proof that you are *not* weak. If you were, he wouldn't be alive."

"But I couldn't save her." Her whispered admission allowed the guilt to almost swallow her whole.

David's head shook slowly. "Oh, girl." His face pinched for several seconds before he gazed deep into her eyes. "Nothin' coulda saved her."

"But..."

"Nothin', Charlotte." Her eyes widened when he said her name, and she swallowed hard. Could it be true?

He grasped her chin and forced her gaze. "We will all grieve her loss. She will always be a missing part of your family. But never, for a second, think you have failed. Every time you think about it, look at Paul, and you will know the truth."

Charlotte nodded as he grunted and pulled her in for one last massive hug as she allowed the comforting heat to infuse her soul. "Never forget." He gruffly whispered into her ear before he stepped back. He slapped Jacob on the shoulder before he made his way up the stairs.

Chapter 7- Before

Her mother's keening wails woke her in the dark of the shelter. Charlotte tensed in her bed. Her small hands gripped the quilt as she listened for other signs of danger. Hearing nothing but the panting breaths of her mother in the next room, Charlotte stepped carefully to the door and peeked at her mother.

Her mother rocked on the edge of the bed. Sweat dripped from her body, and her bottom half was dark with a strange wetness.

Charlotte froze as she made eye contact with her mother. "It's time," said her mother. Charlotte groaned as she rolled over to lay on the bed.

Charlotte rushed around the room like she had learned in the last few weeks. Throwing logs in the stove, she blew on the coals, coaxing it back to life. She poured water and placed the pan on the stove. Grabbing towels and a lantern, she raced back to her mother's side.

Charlotte dabbed lightly on her mother's forehead. The sweat rapidly replaced the dry spot she had just made. She then lit the lamp and placed it on the stand beside the bed.

Her eyes widened as she looked down. Crimson stained her mother's skirt. Dark puddles of red littered the mattress beneath her mother's roiling body. Charlotte swallowed hard as she gently lifted her mother's skirt. A sick feeling coated her body as she placed her hand on her mother's belly, waiting for the tension.

Her mother moaned deeply with short, heaving breaths as Charlotte felt the contraction rip through her mother's body. Dribbles of blood poured from between her legs, so Charlotte grabbed several towels and arranged them underneath.

With each convulsion, the towels became a sopping mess. Charlotte changed them out frequently, all the while praying her mother would be okay. But with each contraction, her mother's body slumped further into the mattress. Huge heaving breaths accompanied her weakening groans. Minutes passed like hours as Charlotte waited for the imminent screech of her mother's wailing moans.

Charlotte sat up straight as her mother's voice changed with the next travail. Her mother's body tensed as she carefully brought her legs closer to her chest. She watched in horror and awe as her mother bore down.

A small hairy dome appeared. Charlotte leaped to her feet and gathered a fresh towel and warm water. She gently wiped as her mother pressed through the pain. Moans changed to wails as her brother's head appeared. His mouth and nose were covered in a crimson viscous liquid.

Charlotte gently suctioned the goop off her brother's mouth and nose. On the next contraction, her brother slipped out into her waiting hands. She carefully pulled him up and rubbed his back as his wailing cries poured through the now-silent room.

She placed him gently upon his mother's chest as she detached the cord. Liquid substance continued to pour in larger quantities from between her mother's legs. Charlotte swallowed hard as she pulled her eyes to meet her mother. Her mother's weak hand gently caressed her baby brother's tiny, unprotected body. His cries were reduced to whimpers as her wan face produced a small smile.

"Beautiful, Paul." Her mother's breathy voice caressed the air. Charlotte moved to her mother's head, and her mother grasped her tightly. "Protect him, Charlotte. Take care of him. Don't let anyone break you apart. Do you hear me?"

Charlotte nodded as she placed a small soft blanket over her brother's small body, watching his tiny body heaving with breath. His lips pursed as he sucked lightly. He was beautiful. Her heart seized as she looked up. Tears blinded her vision, and her petite body quaked. She gently shook her mother's shoulder and managed to displace her hand from her son's back. The hand fell to the mattress with an unrelenting thud that seemed to echo through the room.

Charlotte screamed. "Mama!" She shook her shoulder again and again. Tears poured from her eyes as she looked between Paul and her mother. "Mama?" She grabbed her hand and placed her fingers on her wrist. Nothing. She pulled Paul off her chest and gently placed him in the bassinet on the side. Leaning her head to her mother's chest, Charlotte desperately sought the steady beating of her now absent heart.

She fell to the floor as wracking sobs poured from her body. She clutched her mother's hand as her body quaked with unrelenting tremors.

Her mind swirled through everything. *Protect him. Take care of him.* Thoughts popped through her brain as she looked back at Paul. She stared at her brother without a clue of how to care for him.

She watched his eyes open, and cries that could rival a wailing siren filled the air. Charlotte snapped back to reality as she gathered his tiny body and carefully pulled the blanket around him. His lips pursed as he lightly sucked in the air before his mouth wailed another piercing cry.

She quickly ran to the shelf, gathered some of their stockpiled formula, and warmed a bottle. As she placed it on Paul's lips, he sucked it down speedily. Milk dribbled along his chin as he chugged half the bottle down. She gently pulled it from his lips and placed him against her shoulder. A large belch escaped his body before he cried again. She quickly turned him over and gave him the remainder of his bottle.

A warm wetness gathered near her belly, and she pulled him away from her. Despite the last few hours, she scrunched her nose as she placed him gently on the changing table. She quickly grabbed a diaper before the second part of this disgusting equation would happen.

She wrapped him in a clean blanket and gently placed him in the bassinet. His lips sucked lightly in his sleep as his chest moved with each breath.

Charlotte watched him for several minutes. Her little mind reeling. Panic and fear clawed at her with vicious talons as she considered the daunting task ahead. Her mental to-do list grew exponentially as she tried to comprehend her situation.

Boots echoed from above, and her chest stiffened as she listened carefully. A slow series of knocks eased the tension that had invaded her body moments before. Steps sounded on the stairs as Jacob made his way down to her.

His eyes widened as he gazed. Charlotte looked down and swallowed hard. Large splotches of crimson dotted her nightgown. The wet spot, cold against her skin, was translucent in the lantern light.

Charlotte ran out of the room and donned a clean dress before placing her hands in cool water beside her mother's bed. The water turned pink as she scrubbed her hands, and pink suds gathered on the soap before she stood. Her body froze. Short breaths exited her body as she looked at her mother's body.

A sharp gasp shook her from her stare. Jacob swiftly entered the room and grabbed her mother's wrist. He held his fingers against it before placing them against her neck. Slow tears coursed down Charlotte's cheeks as she watched her friend desperately search for any signs of life.

"Charlotte." His voice squeaked with restrained tears as he knelt in front of her. He pulled her gently against his body, and she sagged as the torrent of restrained grief released in keening wails. Her body shook violently as every ounce of tension poured out.

They stayed that way for a long time as her body seized and spasmed with each wracking heave, wrapping around his like a koala.

He stood with her in his arms before gently placing her in a rocking chair in the corner of the room. He walked out briefly before returning with two quilts and putting one on top of Charlotte's body. The warmth seeped through her as he tucked it gently around her. She shivered lightly as her body accepted the strange warmth. Jacob smirked as he tucked her hair gently behind her ears. Charlotte attempted a small smile despite the overwhelming grief that rested just beneath the surface.

Jacob stood and laid the blanket over her mother. He carefully covered every inch of exposed skin, almost like she was sleeping. Then he closed his eyes with his head bowed. His lips moved with silent words before he sighed and stood.

A small cry pierced the silent air, and Jacob stiffened. *Paul.* Charlotte jumped from the chair and raced to the other room as his cries intensified. Charlotte reached into the bassinet. She fit his tiny body gently against her chest as she tried to figure out what he needed. She placed her finger against his mouth and smiled as he sucked against it gently before letting out another wailing cry.

Charlotte glanced up and saw Jacob staring down at Paul in her arms. She quickly made up a bottle of formula without waiting for an answer. Shaking it, she glanced over at Jacob. Charlotte rocked slowly in place as she fed Paul for the second time that night. "Paul seems to be a good eater already. I think he will do well if we can make this food last. Mama and Daddy stored a lot of..." She swallowed hard as reality crashed over her.

Jacob jumped up and grabbed Paul from her arms as her body cascaded to the floor. The tears poured from her eyes as she pounded against the floor. Daddy was gone. Mama was gone. Everyone had left her alone. She sobbed uncontrollably. Her vision blurred as she thought about everything that she had lost.

She once wanted to be a writer. In her old room above, she had many journals filled with tales of danger, deceit, mystery, and murder. Her heart longed to return to a different world where she could escape for a little while.

A small whimper pulled her back. Jacob rocked awkwardly with Paul in his arms. Her chest squeezed as she thought of everything she would need to do. Tears leaked down her face as doubt invaded her mind.

Large arms encircled her body and lifted her from the floor. She swallowed hard as Jacob placed her gently on the couch. A quilt was pulled around her shoulders before he thrust a cup of tea into her hands. Warmth seeped into her while she stared into the distance. Her mind whirled with near-impossible tasks.

A heavy weight next to Charlotte pulled her away from her errant thoughts. She forced a lump down her throat as he glanced around their shelter. "So, what are you going to do?"

Charlotte's brow turned down at the question. "What do you mean?"

"I mean. What happens now? You know, with your dad somewhere out there and your mom..." Charlotte's heart sank at the thought of being alone in this world. "I mean, Dad would gladly take you..."

Charlotte shrugged. "I don't know." She looked around at the supplies lining the shelves. They would last for a while, but eventually, they would run out. What would she do then?

Jacob placed his arm around her as she placed her head on his shoulder. His warmth and calming presence soothed her frayed nerves. He grabbed the mug, put it on the side table, and settled her in front of him on the couch as she gave into exhaustion.

Movement shook her from her sleep. She peered through heavy lids to watch Jacob slowly move away. She shivered from the heat loss as she burrowed deeper into the blanket. Mama would be up soon to make breakfast. She closed her eyes and drifted off.

A small whimper pulled her from oblivion. Reality crashed into her as she heard Jacob cooing. She immediately jumped from her cocoon and got tangled in the quilt at the thought of Paul. She desperately tried to pull her hands free as the floor grew larger in her vision. She twisted as her shoulder thumped against the floor. Pain seared through her arm as a wail echoed in the space.

Within seconds, large hands scrambled to untangle the blankets. As Charlotte's hands were freed, she grasped her arm, causing shooting pains to shoot through her shoulder. "Ahhhh!"

"Shit," Jacob muttered as he pulled the remaining blankets from around her legs. "Charlotte." She swung her tired eyes to face him as she cradled her arm against her chest. "I'm gonna pick you up, okay?" She nodded. Jacob's arms cradled her. She fought the urge to squirm as pain ran through every part of her body. He gently lifted her and placed her on the couch. Her stomach turned as he lifted his hands from beneath her. Her breath heaved as she clutched her arm against her, fighting against the pain.

"Charlotte." Jacob pulled her attention away from the pain. "I need to get my dad."

She nodded. Gritting her teeth against the pain, she looked over at Paul. Jacob followed her line of sight and clenched his jaw. "What...about...Paul?" she asked out through her teeth.

Jacob shook his head. "I can't take him with me."

"Bring the bassinet over here. I will try to keep him calm."

Jacob's jaw ticked as he looked back and forth between her and Paul. "I don't know..."

"I can do it," Charlotte said as she attempted to raise herself. She froze as a searing pain tore through her body. Swallowing hard, she pushed into a seated position. "Bring him over here," she said, pointing to the space in front of the couch.

Jacob's shoulders sank as he moved to the bassinet. Paul whimpered after he placed it down. "I'll be really quick," he said, kissing her cheek and moving out of the shelter.

Charlotte gently stroked Paul's cheek. His small head turned as he made suckling noises. A small smile stretched across her face. She swallowed hard as her mind wandered to the other room. Her mother would never watch Paul grow. She would never know the joy that he would bring.

She forced a lump down her throat as her mind brought her back to reality. She was left with this responsibility that she never asked for. Tears leaked down her cheeks as she mourned the loss of her childhood.

Bootsteps jarred her from her inner musings. David barreled down the stairs and threw open the door. He fell against the doorjamb as he looked inside the room. His hand went through his hair as he slowly entered the room.

Jacob came over and sat down next to Charlotte. The movement jarred her arm, and Charlotte screamed out in pain. She pulled her hand away from Paul and pulled her arm against her body.

Paul was startled by the movement and cried out. Jacob winced as he pulled Paul from the bassinet. He rocked him slowly while cooing, but Paul wasn't having it. His wail increased in volume as David returned to the room.

Walking over to Jacob, David lifted Paul into his arms. His body looked extra tiny in his massive limbs. He gently transferred Paul to one arm as he walked over to the shelf. He adeptly made a bottle with one hand and cooed gently at him. Charlotte watched in awe as David quickly fed Paul.

Jacob stood and moved the bassinet back to its place against the wall as David finished burping him. When David finished, he gently placed Paul into bed before turning to Charlotte. "Well, girl. Whadya do to yourself?" He kneeled in front of her and pulled her hand off her arm. He shook his head as he gently probed her shoulder. Charlotte winced with each touch. "It looks like you dislocated it." He grimaced as he pulled his fingers away. "I'm going to need to reset it. But it's going to hurt."

Charlotte swallowed hard as he turned to Jacob. "Can you get some cloth for a sling?" Jacob nodded as he moved to the other room. David turned back before he grasped her wrist. His eyes met hers as he extended her arm forward with a sharp motion. She screamed as she felt her shoulder pop. He placed her arm against her chest. Tears streamed down her face as the pain subsided.

Jacob returned and handed David a few strips of cloth. David looped them around her arm and neck, securing them with a knot beneath her arm. Charlotte winced at the movement but was relieved as the pain lessened.

"You need to wear the sling for a few weeks." He looked back over to Paul, sleeping soundly in the bassinet. "It's going to make taking care of him difficult." She nodded as she thought of her alternatives. "I think you need to move in with us."

Charlotte sat back and made eye contact with David. "But Daddy made me promise..."

"I know what you promised. But he isn't here." He motioned around the room and said, "How are you going to take care of all of this?"

Charlotte sat up. "I don't know! Okay!" She forced her chin to her chest as tears slid down her cheeks. She didn't know how but didn't want to break a promise.

David's shoulder slumped as he tipped her face up. "Charlotte. I get it. But don't you think survival is more important than a promise?" His grumbling voice seemed softer in complete contrast to his face.

Charlotte swallowed again as she realized that she didn't have an option. Her shoulders slumped as she sat back against the couch. "Yeah," she mumbled as she resigned to her situation.

David nodded and patted her hand. "It's for the best." He got up and looked around the room. "Jacob. Can you go get the truck?" Jacob nodded as he moved up the stairs. "Okay. Whadya need to bring?"

Charlotte shuffled around the room as David packed her and Paul's things. Jacob returned and helped move stuff out of the house. She froze as she stared at the other room. Her chin quivered as she looked back at David. "What about..." She pointed into the room.

David pulled her into his side. "We'll return after you're settled and take care of her." A couple of tears escaped David's eyes as he spoke. She leaned into him, thankful that she had them.

Chapter 8- After

Charlotte scrambled out of bed as a tremor raced through the foundation. The shaking stopped as suddenly as it started, and she stilled. She swallowed hard as she heard deep voices outside her walls. Paul sat up in the bed. "Charwet?" He rubbed the sleep from his eyes.

"Shh. Paul." She quickly grabbed and donned her clothes before reaching for her shotgun by the stairs. She smiled at Paul before motioning for him to get dressed.

The voices grew louder momentarily before she heard the thump of axes against the wood. Her mind sharpened. *Thieves.* Paul sat gingerly against the mattress, and she gave him one last smile before she tiptoed down the stairs.

Charlotte cautiously opened the outside door and peered outside. Several men stood just on the edge of the tree line. Their axes made quick work of the branches of the massive oak tree they felled.

Quietly making her way out the missing door and down the steps, she puffed her body up as much as she could before cocking the shotgun. The axes stopped, and several pairs of eyes gazed in her direction. Pointing the shotgun in front of her, she stalked in their direction.

"Whaddaya, think you're doing!" She bellowed as she continued moving in their direction, desperately hoping they would leave quickly.

Movement out of the corner of her eye forced her to turn in that direction. Arms frantically waved in the air as the man ran in her direction. The sun reflected in her eyes as she lifted her gun to aim at the man.

"Charlotte!" A familiar voice boomed through the pulsing sound in her ears.

She pulled the gun down and raised her hand to block the invading sun so she could see who was calling. She saw Jacob hopping over the branches and quickly placed the gun against the fence before striding toward him.

The wide eyes of several men from the community met her as she made her way toward the tree. A niggling regret crept up her spine as she took in their frightened faces.

"Darn, Charlotte," Jacob said as he rubbed the back of his neck. "You nearly gave us all heart attacks."

She lowered her head before peeking back at the men as several smiled appreciatively. "Well, you all nearly gave me a heart attack, waking to the tremor from all this." Her hand waved at the oak lying across the yard.

Jacob's cheeks pinked a little as he gave her a sheepish smile. "Dad noticed this tree was leaning toward the house yesterday. I was supposed to mention that we would take care of it this morning..."

She chuckled lightly. After everything that happened yesterday, she didn't blame Jacob for forgetting. "Well, I guess I'll put on a coffee pot." The men nodded appreciatively as she turned back toward the house.

She made her way into the house. Paul peeked around the corner dressed in his boots and overalls. She smiled and brushed his hair out of his face. "It's okay, Paul. It was David and Jacob." She turned to the stove and banked the coals as she placed a large pot of water on the top. "Some men are taking down a tree in the backyard."

"Me go?" Paul asked, his eyes sparkling.

She lightly nodded as he jumped up and began running for the stairs. "Wait, Paul." He turned on the bottom step. "The men are working, so you need to stay out of their way. But you can watch, okay?"

"Okay, Charwet. I be good." He nodded rapidly before scrambling down the steps. She chuckled lightly as she turned back to the stove. Realizing they would probably be hungry, she decided to make oatmeal for the men. So, she placed another pot of water on the stove.

She heard David's booming voice, followed by Paul's belly laugh, as she finished stirring the thickening cereal. She grabbed a serving tray from storage and piled bowls, spoons, and cups before transferring the oatmeal to a covered bowl. She poured the coffee into a large pitcher and brought the provisions outside.

Paul sat on David's shoulders as he supervised the other men hacking away at the tree. Jacob removed his shirt, and his chest glistened in the sun, leaving Charlotte's mouth dry as she gazed at him. She swallowed hard as she carefully made her way across the field.

Jacob slammed his ax into the wood when he noticed her struggling with the large, overfilled tray. He jogged in her direction as the rest of the men stopped their work. He smiled brightly as he took in her offerings. "I thought you guys might be getting hungry, and I wanted to apologize for earlier," Charlotte said as she shrugged sheepishly.

"Thank you, Charlotte," Jacob said. He grabbed the tray from her arms as David directed the men to set a makeshift table on the stump of the oak tree. Her stomach fluttered as Jacob easily placed the tray on the stump. His muscles bunched from the work. He turned and met her eyes before she shook her wayward thoughts and went to one of the small stumps surrounding the table.

When everyone had eaten their fill, one of the workers said, "Delicious meal, Ma'am." She nodded as she gathered up the dirty bowls. The men wandered back to the tree and started working again. Paul stood off to the side with a little hatchet in his hand. Jacob was helping him swing it against one of the removed branches.

She smiled as Jacob met her eyes briefly. As she gathered the bowls, David stepped up to her side. "You doin' okay, girl?"

She nodded. "Just got scared, that's all."

He grunted as he went back to help the men. She balanced the dirty dishes on the tray and tried to lift it off the stump. The bowls wobbled dangerously, threatening to fall, and she paused to balance them when a set of arms pulled the tray over her head. Jacob smiled. "Let me help you."

They made their way to the house. Charlotte placed a large pot of water on the stove as Jacob stoked the fire. They worked in a synchronized rhythm that betrayed the years of practice. This dance spoke of their entwined lives.

Charlotte dried the last bowl and placed it on the shelf as Jacob wiped his hands on the other end of the towel. A brilliant smile broke across his face. "Sorry for scaring you this morning."

Charlotte looked away from his smile, which had drawn her in since she was fourteen. Her heart pounded against her chest in a staccato rhythm as she momentarily relived her fear both from now and before. She shivered as she plastered a smile on her face. "It's fine, Jacob."

He grabbed her chin and forced her to meet his face. "No, it's not. I should have told you. Should have..."

"It's okay." She stopped his rambling apologies. "Yes, you should have told me." His face tucked to his chin. "But you didn't mean to scare me. I'm okay."

She nodded, ending the conversation as she grabbed her gardening gloves from the table by the stairs and went to the backyard. The chopping of axes that echoed around the small valley soothed her frayed nerves from the morning.

Paul sat on the stump, watching the men work steadily on the giant tree. The branches had been stripped from the log and piled in a massive mound behind the men. Charlotte assured herself that Paul was safe before she made her way to the large garden plot. Tiny shoots of life cracked the surface of the dry soil.

Charlotte grabbed her buckets and made her way to the hand pump on the side of the house. Sweat gathered on her brow as she filled the basin with cool water. She dunked the buckets and hauled them out of the water. Streams cascaded over the metal and moistened the mossy ground. Charlotte grunted as she lifted the heavy containers back to the garden.

The sun beat straight overhead as she finished watering the rows of tiny plants that pushed from beneath the soil, giving hope for survival for yet another year. Charlotte loved this time of year—the time of renewal and rejuvenation. Despite the hard work needed, she always loved the effort to keep her family alive.

Charlotte glanced up and felt her heart pound heavily. Paul wasn't sitting where she had last seen him on the stump. Her head jerked in multiple directions, searching for his small form among the men.

His belly laugh echoed from around the side of the house. Instantly, she sighed in relief as she watched him run from the house. Jacob chased him, trying to shake water from his head on the little boy. David paused, scooped him up, and placed him on his shoulders as his laugh continued to echo off the trees.

Charlotte smiled widely at the antics of these large men and their evident love for Paul. Her eyes softened as David pulled Paul into his arms and kissed him under the chin, forcing peals of laughter to escape his tiny body.

Jacob stalked into her peripheral vision, and she turned to face him. "Little boy splashed water onto my head as I was stackin' wood in the shed." His broad smile betrayed his true feelings. She giggled as she imagined the scene. Jacob stepped closer, his t-shirt plastered to his chest and his hair dripping from the impromptu shower. A sneaky smile broke over his face. "Oh. You think this is funny?" He motioned to his body, and she squeaked as she nodded widely. He strode toward her, and she jumped back. A giggle escaped her mouth as she moved away from him. "Come give me a hug, Charlotte."

His arms opened as he chased her around the garden. Her laughter escaped as she ran through the rows. Looking back, she saw he was catching up to her, which was a mistake. Her toe caught the hoe, and she fell onto the soft ground. This gave Jacob a chance to catch her, and he pulled her into his chest while picking her up off the ground. The wetness soaked into her back as he pulled her against his body. Her chest and belly ached from the laughter that continued to pour from her body.

He rubbed his chest against her back, and she squirmed against him. He turned her in his arms, and she froze. His broad smile and booming laughter crinkled the corners of his face. Her heart beat hard in her chest as she swallowed hard. When he met her eyes, his laughter faded. They stared for several minutes as his throat bobbed up and down. She licked her lips as his face descended toward her. Their faces moved closer together, almost as if they were simultaneously determining if they should change their relationship this way.

Determination filled Jacob's eyes as he leaned down and almost made contact when freezing water cascaded over them. Jacob dropped her to the ground as Paul's belly laugh reached her ears. She looked over and saw David and Paul high-fiving, with a bucket in his small hands.

Jacob scooped Paul off his father's shoulders. "Oh really, little boy." Paul screeched as Jacob hauled him over to the basin by the pump. His laughs echoed, and several men stopped to watch the scene. Jacob dunked Paul into the water. His laughs continued with several sputters as Jacob pulled him out of the basin. Charlotte laughed as Jacob tickled his little belly. Water ran in streams down both as Jacob blew raspberries against Paul's belly, and breath stuttered as Jacob placed him on his shoulders and started to race around the yard.

David pulled Charlotte against him as they watched the pair play around the yard. She looked up into his dark eyes. "Love you, girl."

"Love you too." She had never been more thankful for her family. Maybe it wasn't by blood, but love coursed through the family she had built after a tragedy.

Chapter 9- Before

Tears dripped down her cheeks as Jacob and David shoveled dirt into the hole. The hole that now contained her mother.

Charlotte moved forward until her toes touched the hole's edge and peered inside. Her comforter, the one her grandmother had made, was at the bottom of the hole, covered in small clumps of dirt.

The men continued pouring loads of dirt over her mother's covered form until she could no longer see the quilt. Tears trailed off her chin, leaving small divots in the dirt. She couldn't take her eyes off the pit like it was pulling her in.

Paul wiggled in her arms. Charlotte stepped back from the pit and pulled the cloth away. His little fists pushed from within the papoose on her chest. Brilliant blue eyes stared up at her. A large yawn overtook his body as he wiggled and leaned back against her chest.

Charlotte adjusted her sling before she stepped back to the edge. Jacob leaned against the shovel and wiped the sweat from his brow, grimacing before closing his eyes. Charlotte swallowed hard as he continued his task.

After about an hour, the job was complete. A mound of dirt covered the site where the pit once resided. Buried beneath layers of dirt rested her mother, a true final resting place.

David stepped forward and stood at their homemade cross. Jacob and Charlotte had spent a few hours yesterday tying the two logs together with twine. Charlotte wrapped the top log with bundles of lavender and placed her mother's cross around the vertical post.

After the post was decorated, Charlotte kneeled in front of the mound. Her eyes closed as she fought the tears that never seemed to stop. Their weight felt like a ton of bricks as she desperately pushed them back.

Her mind wandered to her mother. Her face. Her words. Her broken promises. So many promises that would never come true.

Charlotte's face grew hot as she pounded her fist into the soil. "IT'S NOT FAIR!" she screamed as she continued to beat the soil into a flat surface. "You were supposed to take care of ME!" her voice rose steadily as she dusted her hands off her pants. "Now you left me alone! All alone!" Tears descended in torrents, leaving tiny divots in the dry ground.

A large pair of arms encircled her from behind. Her initial reaction was to throw them off. She didn't need them. She didn't need anyone.

But they persisted. Their steady pressure eased its outward presence, leaving her anger to simmer close under the surface.

Almost as suddenly as the pressure appeared, it released. Charlotte scrambled to her feet, desperate to escape. Her eyes went to the headstone, and she stumbled. Unable to look away.

Her arm encircled Paul as her eyes focused on the cross. Unable to hold it in anymore, a keening wail escaped her as tears streamed down her face.

David approached slowly and pulled Paul from the sling across her chest. His eyes were wide open, and despite her groans, she could see he was also crying.

Her mother was gone. It was final. There was no coming back. Not that she thought it was possible; her mind hadn't wrapped around it until now. She allowed the tears to flow. Allowed herself to feel the desperate pain of losing her family.

She sagged into Jacob's arms. Her stomach cramped, and her head throbbed as she closed her eyes. Sending thoughts to the heavens, hoping they would one day be reunited.

Chapter 10- After

The warm wind whipped through the trees as she grasped the clothespins and secured her shirt on the line. Branches swayed behind her as she hummed through her chore. Her mind wandered back several weeks ago, the day that almost changed everything.

Charlotte didn't know when her feelings for her friend had changed. It had been slow, like molasses on a cold winter morning. He had always been in her life. Her father and David had been best friends almost since their first day in Waltham.

Her father had been mowing the front lawn when David, Helen, and Jacob showed up in their driveway. Charlotte had been playing on the porch with her dolls while watching her father. The screen door had snapped closed, and her mother had come outside. Charlotte had looked up as her father turned off the mower.

"Evening," David said. He took his hat off, revealing his wild hair.

Her father had moved in their direction as her mother urged her to her feet. A frown settled on Charlotte's face as she looked down at her dolls. She wanted to continue playing.

"Evening." Her father moved toward the newcomers. Her mother grabbed her hand and dragged them down the porch stairs.

"I'm David. This is my wife, Helen, and our son, Jacob." He motioned to the little boy hiding behind his mother.

Her father motioned for us to join him. Her mother dragged her onto the lawn. She hid behind her father when they reached him. "Nice to meet you. I'm Glenn. This is my wife, May." He pulled me from behind him. "And this is our daughter, Charlotte."

Jacob peeked from behind his mother, and Charlotte gave him a small smile. "We just set up the swing set in the backyard. Would you like to come back for some iced tea?" My mother asked. Charlotte's eyes widened and swung to her mother. She couldn't believe that she had invited these people into their house.

Her mother had mostly been a homebody on the base. She didn't have people over, and Charlotte didn't mind at the time. But as she went to school, she realized that she didn't know very many kids like the others. She often wondered why but didn't question it.

"That would be nice," Helen said. "I brought some molasses cookies as a welcome gift."

Her mother and Helen started chatting animatedly as they approached the house. "Charlotte," her father mentioned, and she looked up at him. Why don't you show Jacob to the backyard? She nodded slowly, not really wanting to, but knowing it would be better if she followed his suggestion.

She and Jacob made their way silently to the backyard. Charlotte didn't know what to say. It felt awkward being thrown into this playdate. She heard her father's booming laughter behind them and glanced back at the men.

Jacob looked at the ground as they slowly made their way to the swing set her father had built earlier that day. She sat on the swing and started rocking back and forth. Jacob looked up briefly before digging his toe into the dirt beneath the swing.

"So," Charlotte said. "Have you lived here all your life?" She desperately tried to think of something else to say.

"Yup," Jacob said as he swung slowly. Charlotte nodded as she started swinging a little more. "Where'd you move from?" He pushed lightly off the ground.

"Fort Bragg in North Carolina," Charlotte said as she pumped harder. Almost as if he couldn't resist, he pumped his legs, trying to match her speed.

Jacob smiled at her, and she smiled back. "Army brat?" She giggled lightly before nodding. "What made your parents want to move out here?"

She shrugged as she pushed off with more force. "Daddy's from here. His parents owned this place."

His eyes widened. "Your grandparents were Mr. & Mrs. Fletcher?" She nodded with a chuckle.

"Yup. Gran and Gramp died in that accident last year." Her face fell. She didn't know them well, but they were always kind when she saw them. "Daddy left the Army, and my parents decided to move us here."

His eyes fell as she mentioned the accident. "I'm really sorry you lost them. Mrs. Fletcher was my kindergarten teacher. She was amazing."

Charlotte forced a smile onto her face. "It's okay. I didn't know them well. We were always moving, and they couldn't always come to see us." Some of her felt jealous that this boy knew her grandmother better than her.

"That sucks," he said. They continued pumping their legs, almost unconsciously competing with who could fly highest.

Charlotte shrugged. "It's okay. I'm used to it."

They were both silent for several minutes. The small camaraderie they had developed was almost falling away.

"What grade will you be in next year?" he asked, breaking the silence. "3rd."

He smiled. "You'll love Mrs. Young. She's a great teacher who tries to make learning fun."

She smiled and asked, "How about you?"

"4th."

She frowned. "So, we won't see much of each other."

"Naw. It's a small school. We'll see each other." He gestured to the tree line. "You want to check out the woods with me? There's a small pond down back that has tadpoles in it."

"Sure," she said as she jumped off the swing.

"Dad! I'm taking Charlotte to see the pond!"

Charlotte looked back at their fathers sitting in the Adirondack chairs by the firepit. "You keep a close eye on her son! She doesn't know these woods yet!"

"I know, Dad!" He turned and offered his hand. "You ready for an adventure?" She placed her hand in his, and they took off for the woods. She learned every inch of those woods over the next few years with Jacob.

Charlotte shook her head, clearing the memory from her mind. She smiled broadly as she shook the sheet and placed it over the line. Ever since that day, he had been her constant companion. He took care of bullies for her and spent every spare moment he wasn't working on their farm together. It wasn't until everyone disappeared that she could say she looked at Jacob differently. She was surprised when she noticed her stomach twittering, full of butterflies, when she saw him. He had grown up before her eyes, and now she didn't know what to do. She didn't want things to be awkward between them.

She sighed as she put the last bit of laundry on the line. It would be better if they could keep it as just friends. But she didn't know if she could ignore the feelings that bubbled up whenever he was around.

She lifted the basket and went inside, trying to decide what to make for dinner. David had some dried venison for stew. As she walked into the house, she took stock of her supplies.

Chapter 11- After

Charlotte softly hummed as she hit the top step. She had left Paul to take a nap in bed. His naps were becoming less frequent, but she knew he would be growing soon when one came along. She sighed at the thought of the new clothes she would need to make to accommodate his growing body, which flashed through her mind as she placed the basket in the spare room and shut the door.

She turned toward the bed and stepped back. The blankets were askew, but Paul wasn't tangled in them. "Paul! Where are you?" She started looking around, thinking he was playing hide and seek. "I'm going to find you!" she yelled, which would have usually been followed by a giggle. When she paused her search, silence rained around her. A shot of panic coursed through her body as she blinked, trying to think.

Paul didn't usually go far. He might come outside to see what she was doing if she wasn't there when he woke. She made her way down the stairs, her hands trembling as she quickly checked the house. Paul didn't usually hide, but it wasn't unheard of. "Paul! Paul?"

When she heard nothing, she went outside and began calling for him. "Paul? Paul!" She ran around the backyard. Her voice grew hoarse from yelling, but she kept searching. Her panic increased as she didn't discover him in the usual spots.

Jacob came running from the barn. She jumped when he placed his hand on her shoulder. "What's going on?"

"Paul is missing!" she yelled as fear sank deep into her belly. Her head bounced around the area as if it was on a swivel. Her eyes searched the area, and she could not focus on anything for too long. "Paul! You get back here!"

Jacob's shoulders stiffened as he began searching. He turned her around to face him. His fingers went to her chin until she met his eyes. "We'll find him." Charlotte nodded. "I'm going to get Dad, and we will search. Have you checked the house?"

"Yes! I checked everywhere inside," her voice rose in pitch.

He nodded. "Okay. Let me get Dad, and we'll search with you." Her toe tapped the dirt of the driveway as she waited for Jacob and David. Her eyes continued to ping around the area, hoping she would see something.

David and Jacob burst from the barn. His steps thumped against the ground as he stomped across the yard. She became afraid, thinking David was angry with her. She was almost crouched when he stood in front of her. "When was the last time you saw him?" he growled.

She swallowed hard. "I put him down for a nap a couple of hours ago." He nodded. "Then I did some laundry and hung it out to dry. When I brought the basket upstairs, I noticed he was not in bed."

She paused. Her voice was hoarse from all the yelling earlier. "Deep breaths, girl," David said. She inhaled deeply, allowing herself a moment.

"At first, I thought he was playing hide and seek. He likes that game. But he wasn't in the house. So, I came outside and checked all the normal places. He's just gone." Tears streamed down her face as she thought about Paul out there alone.

"Okay, girl. We're going to find him." She gave a slight nod. "Jacob, check the east field. I'll grab a horse and check the north field. Charlotte. You check the west tree line. We'll meet back here in a couple of hours. Shout if you find something."

The three split up, and Charlotte ran from the western tree line. "Paul! Where are you?" She yelled as she followed the edge of the woods. Her eyes jumped back and forth. When she got to the edge of the clearing to the north, something caught the corner of her eye—a piece of fabric swaying in the breeze.

Charlotte tore across the clearing as her feet thumped against the ground. She stopped just before the branch. Swinging in the breeze, the red and blue plaid strip hung trapped in a thorny branch. While this could have been there for a while, she swore she hadn't seen it before.

Looking closer, she noticed the pattern was the same as the shirt she dressed him in earlier that morning.

"Paul! PAUL!!" she yelled as she skirted the edge of the woods. While she was not afraid of the woods, she knew better than going in alone. A small piece of her wanted to charge in and find him, but she knew that wasn't smart. He could be anywhere, and she could easily get lost.

Looking up, she noticed the sun was just past noon. She had several hours before evening fell. "Jacob! David!" she yelled as she paced the tree line, peering into the shadowy depths.

"Charlotte! Where are ya, girl?" David's voice boomed in the distance.

She looked around. "In the clearing! North of the pasture!" she yelled back.

Horse hooves pounded against the ground, shaking the dirt. She turned as Jacob and David rode into the clearing. She froze as she turned toward the woods and saw movement. Her breaths heaved in her chest as a small shadow moved through the forest. The shadow approached, and she swallowed hard. Hope made her chest hurt until the shadow burst into the clearing. A small bleat accompanied the intrusion, and tears streamed down her face. A sheep. A stupid sheep! She panted as her mind whirled at the thought of all the things that could happen to Paul in the woods. While predators were not common in the area, bears were known to roam the woods of the mountain. But foxes, coyotes, and other animals could be dangerous to a small boy.

When Jacob and David arrived, she had worked herself up into a blind panic. "Jacob!" She cried, her voice taking on the edge of dread. She gasped as fear coursed through her. Her breaths came in short pants as darkness edged her vision.

She heard footsteps but couldn't move. "Charlotte! Charlotte!" Jacob's voice pierced her panic as he scooped her into his arms. His warmth seeped into her cold limbs.

"Breathe, girl. Slow, deep breaths," David growled.

Her chest rattled as she pulled a shuddery breath into her lungs. The darkness faded with each breath, but the panic never receded completely. As she relaxed slightly into Jacob's embrace, the scent of pine and sweat soothed her even further. They stood for longer than they should have, but she couldn't let go. Paul was out there, all alone.

"Whaddaya find, Charlotte?" David's voice pierced her receding panic, and she was pulled back to reality. They needed to find Paul.

She pointed at the woods. "Over there, I found a piece of cloth. It was the same as the shirt he had on this morning."

David moved carefully toward the edge of the clearing. Charlotte stood stock still as the men looked around, checking the ground. Charlotte swallowed hard as she watched the men search the area. "Over here!" Jacob yelled as he stood near the roots of a tree.

Charlotte rushed over to that spot, but Jacob stopped her from running. "Whadya find, Jacob."

Jacob pointed to a spot on the ground. "Footprints. Large. Adult. Looks like boots."

David cursed as he walked back to the horses. He fiddled with the saddle as he pulled his rifle from the holster. He loaded the weapon and swung up onto his horse.

"Wha...Wha..." Charlotte said as she stared at David. "What is happening?"

David looked down at her. His eyes creased. "Watchers. I don't know anyone else that would sneak around our property like that."

"Do you mean?" Charlotte felt the panic escalate. Her voice rose as she processed. "They have Paul!"

David nodded. "Jacob. Keep your rifle across your legs and Charlotte behind you."

Charlotte's mind whirled as she looked between the two men. She blinked rapidly as she thought about what that meant for Paul. Jacob pulled on Charlotte's arm and led her to the horse. He helped her into the saddle and swung himself up before her.

They rode slowly into the woods. The sun filtered through the leaves, making her vision hazy. The horses strode slowly through the branches, stepping carefully around the trees.

They continued for a while, pointing out what Charlotte overlooked: broken branches, small footprints, more boot prints, and other signs that someone had been there. The longer they searched, the darker the woods got inside.

They pulled up to a stream that led between two ponds. They allowed the horses to drink as they ate granola bars. Charlotte wasn't hungry but shoved the food down, knowing her body needed it.

"The boot prints lead up the mountain," David said as he pointed up. "There are a lot of caves up there but not much else. Don't know why they'd take him that way. But we're going to have to search on foot. The horses won't make it up that slope."

Jacob chewed slowly. "Do you think they have an outpost up there? So close to us?"

The fear in Jacob's eyes made Charlotte's heartbeat quicken. The Watchers. This close to their farm?

"Don't know. But we need to check it out." David's face looked like stone.

Jacob looked over at Charlotte. "Should Charlotte stay here? It could be dangerous."

Her eyes widened at his words. "No!" she said, scrambling to her feet. "You can't leave me. I need to find Paul."

A hand landed on her shoulder. "Don't worry, girl. We won't leave you, but Jacob has a point. It will be dangerous."

Charlotte straightened her shoulders. "I can shoot. Daddy made sure I knew how to handle a weapon."

Jacob grimaced as she spoke. "I know, Charlotte. But these men are not your normal people. They have military training. You could get hurt."

"So could you! What makes you able to handle it more than me? Because I'm a girl! That's bull."

David chuckled beside her and said, "She's got a point, son." He patted her on the shoulder.

Jacob approached her slowly. "It's not that I don't think you're capable, Charlotte. I just. I don't know what I would do."

Her eyes widened as she swallowed hard. What was he saying? They stood inches apart as she watched the fear skitter across his face.

She grabbed his hand and said, "I can do this, Jacob. I need to do this." Her voice was softer.

She watched his throat bob before he nodded. He walked back to his horse and pulled a revolver from the saddle. He placed it in her hand and instructed, "Don't forget that if you decide to shoot. Shoot to kill."

Goosebumps rose on her arms and neck as she gripped the weapon. The cold metal bit into the soft skin of her hand. Her chest tightened as she raised it to make sure it was loaded.

She nodded as she looked between the two men bracketing her. They turned and hiked slowly up the steep embankment.

Chapter 12

Voices grew louder as they hiked higher into the woods. The light was barely visible over the horizon as David squatted behind a tree. "We should wait here until dark," he whispered as he turned his ear toward the voices. Jacob kneeled beside him as he pulled Charlotte between them.

A loud, angry voice rose above the other. "We need to move him at dawn. They'll search for him, and we must be gone by morning."

Charlotte's heart beat faster in her chest. Were they talking about Paul? Hope surged through her as she looked at Jacob. His finger came up to his lips, and she nodded.

"Why's he so important, sir?" another voice rang out.

"He's their leader's little boy," the voice chuckled. "He will do anything to keep him safe."

A third voice entered the conversation. "Are you sure, sir? I mean. This is a lot of risk."

"I'm sure. King will be putty in our hands when he finds out." Several feet shuffled at his words. "We need to take watches. Casper and Knight."

"Yes, sir."

"You've first watch. Howe and I will take the second watch. Be on the lookout. Hopefully, they won't find us, but we need to be prepared in case they do."

"Yes, sir."

Four men. Four armed men guarded someone in one of the caves. Was it Paul? It had to be. But who was this King? And why would he care?

David motioned for them to move down the hill a little bit. He led them carefully over the rocks in silence. When they entered a different cave, they had checked earlier, Charlotte let out a breath she didn't know she was holding.

"Do you think it's Paul?" she whispered as Jacob pulled water and some jerky from his backpack. He thrust some into her hands as he placed his pack behind a rock in the cave.

David nodded as he tore a piece of his jerky off. He swallowed quickly. "Yup. Their leader is worried that we'll find him. So, we need to get him tonight."

"How are we going to do that?" Charlotte looked between the two men as she tore a piece of jerky off and chewed, allowing the spicy texture to run down her throat.

Jacob said, "We're going to have to create a distraction—something to get most of the guards out of the way. That way, we can get him out quickly."

David nodded. He pulled a map from his pocket and spread it on the rock. "They're in this cave," he said, pointing to a place on the map. "Over here is another cave about half a mile away from their cave. If we start a fire in that cave, the wind should push the smell up to them. Hopefully, that will draw at least two away from the cave."

Charlotte nodded as she studied the features on the map. She looked up at David in admiration. Clearly, he had scouted the woods and knew a lot about the area. David looked down at her and gave her a small smile.

"Jacob. Head to this cave in a few hours. Start a fire and wait for it to catch before heading back here. We should wait for their second watch. If we can lure their leader away, it would be better. Charlotte and I will head up to the cave. We can sneak into the cave and pull Paul out when they leave the area."

The blood drained from Jacob's face. He looked back and forth between his father and Charlotte. "But..."

David touched Jacob's shoulder and said, "I know you want to protect her, son. But we need to split up; she is the smallest and lightest. She can get into the cave and carry Paul out."

Jacob nodded before he moved toward her. He put his arm around her as she laid her head against his shoulder. Charlotte swallowed hard. "It's going to be okay, Jacob," she whispered as he laid his lips against her head and pulled tighter against his side.

"I know. I just..." He turned her head so their eyes met. "I can't lose you, Charlotte. You're important to me, and I don't know..." His throat bobbed.

She placed her hand on his face. "I get it, Jacob. I will be careful, and your father will keep me safe."

He closed his eyes. Tears welled in her eyes. She shouldn't promise anything because something could happen to them. Any of them, and she couldn't lose any more of her family. Her heart couldn't take it.

Silence reigned for several minutes before she remembered something they had overheard. She looked over at David, who stared out the cave entrance. "David," she whispered as Jacob lifted his head off her. David turned to face her. "Who do you think King is?"

David shrugged. "Don't know, Charlotte. But that man seems to think it's Paul's father."

Charlotte pulled back suddenly. "Daddy? But he's been gone for four years. There's no way."

Despite keeping hope for a long time, Charlotte realized that her father was most likely dead. She hadn't heard from him since that last phone call. At the time, it had hurt deeply to let him go. To let hope go. But it was necessary for her sanity.

"I know it seems impossible. But that man thinks Paul is King's son for some reason."

Charlotte swallowed hard. Was it possible that her father was still alive? If he was, why hadn't he contacted them? Why hadn't he come home? She shook her head to clear the thoughts of her father away. It didn't matter right now. Now, they needed to rescue Paul.

"You two should get some sleep. It's going to be a long night."

Jacob nodded as he pulled her back against the wall of the cave. Her arm broke out in goosebumps as she rested it against the cold rocks. In contrast, her other arm rested against Jacob's warm body. She wrapped her arm around Jacob's body to stay warm. Jacob huffed as he pulled her tighter into his embrace. "Sleep," he whispered, sending chills down her spine. She closed her eyes in the hope that sleep would come.

~~~~~~~

Charlotte woke with a start as Jacob released her against the rocks. She shuddered as the infusion of cold skittered across her body. She leaped from the rocks and gasped loudly, echoing in the cave.

Jacob and David stared at her with their fingers against their lips. Heat suffused her face as she lowered her eyes to the ground. Shame mixed with guilt swirled around the pit of her stomach like a tornado.

Jacob slowly made his way to the back of the cave. He lifted her chin with his knuckle. "It's okay, Charlotte," he whispered, lowering his lips against her cheek.

"You're leaving?"

He nodded. "I'll see you back here in a few hours." Not leaving any room for argument.

She threw her arms around his shoulders and hugged him tightly. "You better come back to me," she whispered.

"Yes, ma'am," he whispered as he kissed her again on the cheek and stepped to the edge of the cave. He hugged his father. David whispered something indiscernible in his ear. Jacob nodded before he slipped into the darkness.

An ache bloomed in Charlotte's chest as she lost sight of him a few feet from the cave entrance. Worry settled into her chest, causing it to tighten. She prayed for his safety as David motioned her closer.

"We'll give him a few minute's head start, but soon, we need to move up toward the camp." Charlotte nodded as she stared out into the darkness. "He'll be okay." He laid a kiss on her head.

Charlotte looked into David's eyes and said, "They both will."

He gave her a wry smile and squeezed her shoulder. The next few minutes felt like an eternity. No matter how much she needed to rescue Paul, a part of her longed for her room at the farmhouse. For the warmth, comfort, and safety it provided.

After an interminable time, David tapped her shoulder and motioned her outside. They climbed the rocks slowly under the moonlight. She cringed when a stick cracked beneath her feet or her shoes slipped against the stones. She hoped the frogs croaking in the forest masked it.

David pulled her to a stop at the base of some trees about 200 yards from the camp—a small fire burned in the entrance to the cave. Small bursts of light cascaded in random spurts against the cave wall, illuminating two men in full military gear.

She silently waited as she watched one of the men nod forward before shooting up suddenly. They were tired. David gave her a thumbs up.

One of them stood suddenly, looking away from them. "Howe. Get up."

The other man stood slightly wobbly on his feet. "Yes, sir." His voice was raspy, as if he was just waking up.

"Get Casper." He pointed in the other direction. "Smoke coming from that direction."

"Do you think it's them?"

The man smirked in the firelight. "Yes."

Howe scrambled into the cave and returned a minute later with another man. "Okay, boys. Let's go hunting." He rubbed his hands together as he grabbed a rifle off the rocks and headed slowly through the woods toward the other cave.

Charlotte swallowed hard, praying that Jacob was on his way back to the cave. David tapped her shoulder and motioned for them to walk toward the cave. She skirted the entrance and peered around the edge. The small fire didn't allow much light, but she saw a bleary-eyed man with a weapon sitting beside another smaller figure lying very still against the rock. His hands were bound in front, and a gag was in her mouth.

But she recognized the red and blue plaid print. She almost gasped aloud and shoved her fist into her mouth to stop her from calling out. She stepped back, allowing David to peek inside.

He stepped back before he picked up a rock and tossed it toward the woods. The rock cracked against the ground. Seconds later, the bleary-eyed man ran outside the cave. His movements were sluggish as he stumbled out of the entrance.

David moved behind him and slammed the butt of his rifle against his head. Charlotte watched the man's eyes roll into the back of his head as he crumpled like a folding fan.

Charlotte winced as his head bounced against a tree root. When he eventually woke up, that was going to hurt.

David kneeled next to him and checked his pulse. He gave a thumbs up, and Charlotte released her breath. As much as she hated these men for taking Paul, she wouldn't wish death upon them. They deserved to suffer.

Charlotte raced into the cave. Paul didn't move, and her heart stuttered as she kneeled beside him. His pulse beat slowly against her. His skin was cold, and his lips were blue. Charlotte pulled a hissing breath through her teeth. Maybe they did deserve death.

She pulled him into her arms and shivered as her skin met his. His little eyes opened slightly, and he mumbled against the gag. She shook her head and placed her finger against her lips.

His lashes fluttered closed. Charlotte winced and walked carefully out of the cave. David motioned for her to move quickly, and then he grabbed Paul from her and carried him down over the rocks.

They made their way down the rocks as quietly as possible. David took several different turns as he cradled a limp Paul against his chest.

"Hoo Hoo...Hoo Hoo..." David said as they approached the cave.

Jacob came running out and pulled Charlotte into his arms. He rubbed his hands over her head and kissed her against the crown. "Thank God. I was getting worried."

Charlotte pushed him away and grabbed his hand as David waited for them a little way down. "We've got to go. Paul needs to get warm."

Jacob slung his pack across his shoulders and started down the hill. As they hit the bottom, a loud voice screamed from above them. Charlotte stopped dead in her tracks and turned toward the top.

"They know," David said as he pulled himself onto his horse. "We need to go."

Jacob grabbed Charlotte and threw her on his horse before pulling himself behind her. David took off toward the farm with Paul. Jacob spurred his horse, and they galloped into the trees. She peeked behind her up the hill and could swear she saw a man tear through the trees, exiting near where they had left moments before. She shivered against Jacob as he broke through the tree line into the clearing where their adventure had started.

Chapter 13

They raced through the woods. Small branches smacked their faces, but nothing phased Charlotte. She needed to get home and get Paul warm. Nothing else mattered at that point as they broke free of the trees.

Jacob pulled up to the pump beside the house. David's horse was already drinking water from the basin. Jacob pumped a few more pulls into the basin for his horse, but Charlotte didn't wait for him. She raced into the house and went up the stairs. David was getting the fire going on the stove. She desperately searched for Paul and found him beneath several blankets on the bed.

"He needs body heat, girl. I stripped his clothes, but he needs you beneath there with him." She nodded as she climbed beneath the covers and pulled Paul's cold body against her. She could feel the cold radiating from his tiny body, and she was amazed he was alive.

"Ch...Cha...Charwet..." Tears ran down his cheeks as he shivered violently against her body.

She pulled him closer to her body. "Oh, Paul. I am so glad that you are safe. I love you." His eyes were closed, and small puffs of air pushed against her chest. Another set of arms encircled them under the blankets. Jacob bracketed Paul between them, giving him the life-giving heat he needed.

David stoked the fire, almost making Charlotte sweat beneath the covers. "Let's check his temperature," he said as he pulled the glass thermometer. "I checked him when I got here. Even after riding under my sweatshirt, he was 95.6."

Charlotte swayed in the bed. He was hypothermic. "We got him, Charlotte," Jacob said as he kissed his head softly. "He's safe." She nodded as she peeled the blanket away from him. He violently shivered as they checked his temperature.

"96.6. Good. He's going up, but we aren't out of the woods yet," David said as he pulled the blankets up around us. When he wakes, we need to get some warm fluids into him. Do we have any broth left?"

"In the pantry, there should be a jar of chicken broth on the shelf." David nodded, moving toward the door. His feet stomped rapidly down the stairs. She turned and placed her lips against Paul's head and finally allowed the grief out. Tears leaked down her cheeks as she rocked his small body against hers. Jacob tightened his grip around her body and kissed her forehead. She looked up into his eyes and saw the pain reflecting in them. Charlotte licked her lips, tasting salt from her tears. He rested his lips against her forehead, and she closed her eyes, soaking in the comfort he was providing.

"Charwet." His small voice woke her, and she smiled. His body still trembled, and she pulled the blankets around them. Jacob lay on the pillow, his arms still encasing them in warmth. He opened his eyes, and she gasped at the intensity in them.

"Good. He's awake," David said as he moved to the stove. He pulled a bowl of broth from the pot, sitting off to the side. "Let's check his temperature and get him to sip on the broth." Charlotte nodded, stripping the blankets off them.

"97.2. That's good. A little broth should help him feel better. I'm sure he's thirsty."

"Firsty," Paul said with a nod.

Charlotte chuckled a little. "Okay. Let's get some broth into you." David handed her a mug, and she helped Paul drink the warm liquid. The worst of his shivers had subsided, and the pink glow of his cheeks was returning.

"Here's some stew, girl," David said as he handed her a bowl. "Why don't you eat, and we'll get some clothes for Paul." At first, Paul clung to Charlotte almost like he didn't want her out of sight.

"It's okay, Paul. I am going to be right over there," she said as she pointed to the couch. He blinked and then slowly released his grip. She smiled on the outside as David grabbed some pajamas, but inside, she was screaming. Where was her independent and vibrant little boy? The one who took his first steps in the garden trying to grab a pea pod off the vine. Or who growled at the neighborhood dog when he got too close? The little boy who never failed to get muddy in the spring and loved to catch snowflakes on his tongue. She just prayed that he would find his way back.

Paul clung to Jacob as Charlotte spooned stew into her mouth. It was hot and probably burned her tongue, but she couldn't find it in herself to care. She just watched as her boy retreated into himself. Jacob held him against his chest and rubbed his back, placing kisses against his head. She had to look away before the tears started falling again.

She stirred her stew slowly, taking a spoonful now and then. The couch dipped with weight. "You should eat," Jacob said as he spooned in a mouthful. Charlotte giggled as some of the stew dribbled out of his mouth. "God, that's hot."

She finally looked up and saw David snoring on the bed with Paul on his chest. The blanket was pulled up around them, and Paul was snuggled in deep. She could imagine everyone was tired. It had been a long day.

She laid her head against Jacob's shoulder and ate the rest of her stew. They sat in silence punctuated by the sudden snores from the bed. Jacob placed their bowls on the side table before returning to the couch. His arm went around her and pulled her against his chest. Her belly fluttered with the contact. She laid her head against his chest and listened to the soothing beat of his heart. His pine scent enveloped her as he stroked her head.

"You know, I could get used to this." He snuggled deeper into her arms.

She smiled up at him. "Mmmhmm."

"Charlotte." He gazed down at her with soft eyes. "There is something I have been wanting to do." Her eyes widened as he smiled down at her. "I know this is probably the worst possible time. But I may never get the courage if I don't do this now." She swallowed hard as butterflies took flight in her stomach. Her heart pounded fiercely in her chest.

He leaned down and pressed his lips gently against hers. They rested there for a few moments before he began to move them. The belly flutters increased as he gently stroked his callused finger against her cheekbones. She shivered against him as he rested his forehead against hers.

"That was amazing," he whispered as his lips ghosted along hers one last time.

She smiled brightly. "Yeah. It was." She sighed and snuggled into his side. Her eyes closed as she relished the warmth of his arms.

Chapter 14

Charlotte tugged against the rugged root that burrowed through her garden row, the roots choking out the nutrients intended for her vegetables. Without the garden, they wouldn't survive the winter. Small pieces of leaf fell off with each pull. Finally, the root gave way; she fell with an "oomph," her arms flailing to brace for impact.

A giggle rose from the other end of the row. Paul's little shoulders shook with glee as he glanced in her direction. She narrowed her eyes, and he shut his mouth, but his shoulders shook.

A chuckle escaped her mouth as she slowly rose, taking stock of her body. "You think that is funny?" His head moved up and down rapidly as he lost the battle with his laughter. "Oh really?" She scooped him off the ground and tickled him on his sides. He squirmed, releasing streams of laughter.

Charlotte smiled as she placed Paul on the ground. He scrambled away from her, but as she squatted down to his level, he threw his tiny body against her. His small arms and legs wrapped around her body like a spider monkey. He had been unusually clingy in the last week since his abduction. Charlotte hoped he would eventually return to the independent, happy little boy she knew. She knew this would take time, but there was a possibility that he would always be different—a tear gathered in her eye as she mourned the loss of his innocence.

Nobody had come onto their property; they had been watching. Jacob and David took turns at night. They both rode the fence line together. But there hadn't been any sign of The Watchers that took Paul.

A small part of Charlotte was worried. She didn't know what that could mean for them. They wouldn't have given up after the lengths they had gone to get Paul.

Paul had told them what he remembered from that day. He had woken from his nap and came outside to find her. When he got close to the barn, he saw a loose lamb. He had followed it toward the woods, and that was when the men had grabbed him. He didn't remember much after that, except that he was cold. The three of them had stayed up late one night talking about it. They didn't have lambs on the farm. They assumed the men had stolen the lamb and brought it to entice Paul toward the woods. And it worked.

His body grew heavy in her arms, and she knew he was asleep. While his time for regular naps had faded in the last year, Paul had been more tired than usual since his adventure. She lifted him and slowly made her way into the house. She placed his body, softened by sleep, into the bed and brushed her lips across his head. He squirmed slightly but settled quickly. Charlotte brushed his bangs from his face and kissed his forehead.

Charlotte wished her to-do list was shorter so she could stay at Paul's side, but the garden wouldn't take care of itself. She sighed as she pulled herself to stand, stretching lightly before taking one last look at Paul. His body was already sprawled across the mattress. Charlotte smiled before making her way out back.

She pulled buckets of composted soil from her pile, which had deteriorated over the past year. Hoisting the yoke across her back, she paused, her breath heaving through her pinched mouth as she adjusted the load across her shoulders. Slowly making her way across the yard, she maneuvered through the various rows and dropped the load to the ground.

Rolling her shoulders, she gazed around at the small plants poking from beneath the soil. She located cucumbers, peppers, zucchini, and small tomato plants. Pride flowed through her as she surveyed her garden.

She kneeled at the next row and turned the soil, adding compost to keep the land fertile. She didn't know how long the garden would be needed to survive, possibly the rest of her life. Once the row was turned correctly, she began planting the beans. She had started them in the sunroom a few weeks earlier. The little shoots poked out of the soil and stretched toward the sun.

Charlotte worked furiously to get the rest of the plants in the ground before Paul woke up: she was afraid he would be scared if he woke up alone. Wiping the sweat off her brow as she finished planting that row, she noticed the sun hanging high in the sky, and her stomach rumbled.

Her knees creaked as she stood for the first time in a while. Charlotte took off her gloves and wiped the stray dirt from her pants. She entered the sunroom and watered her pumpkin and potato seedlings before going upstairs.

Paul was still sleeping when she entered. She went back down to the kitchen and started the fire. Placing the stew on to warm, she moved back toward the counter, pulling the bread dough she had made earlier from the cupboard. She pressed flour into the dough and kneaded it against a wooden board.

Jacob stomped into the kitchen, his forehead dotted with sweat. Charlotte looked away as he entered. Things had been awkward between them since that night, despite knowing her feelings weren't one-sided. Charlotte struggled to wrap her mind around their relationship.

He was her best friend, and she didn't want to lose that, but she didn't know how to deal with the feelings swirling through her belly whenever she saw him.

She glanced over as she pressed her fingers into the dough, allowing it to ooze over the top. Jacob lifted a glass of water, and she lost focus on her task as she watched his throat bob with each swallow.

She bit her bottom lip as he lifted the bottom of his T-shirt and wiped his forehead. Her legs weakened, and she grabbed the counter for support. Her heart pounded in her chest as he turned toward her and smiled.

"Charlotte. Can we take a walk?"

She shook her head and focused on her task, kneading the dough for several minutes, hoping he would leave. Heat suffused her face, the hair on the back of her neck pricked, and she felt him behind her. She shaped the dough and placed it in the bread pans.

She wiped her hands on her apron before placing the bread in the oven. Afterward, she set one of those old kitchen timers and put it on the counter.

Jacob grabbed her wrist as she reached for a cloth to wipe the counters. She swallowed hard as she pulled her arm from his grasp. She turned and met his eyes. "Please. I just...I need to talk to you."

His voice was gritty like sandpaper, and she sighed. "I can't right now. Paul's napping upstairs. I can't leave him alone. Plus, I just put the bread in and don't want it to burn." She had a million excuses: things she needed to do—anything but have this conversation.

Jacob nodded before putting his finger up; he moved quickly out of the door while she tapped her foot lightly against the floor. Several minutes later, David walked through the door. "Girl. Put my son out of his misery and talk to the boy. I'll keep an ear out for Paul and take the bread out."

Charlotte chuckled as she wiped her hands on a towel and removed her apron. She walked over to David and kissed him on the cheek.

Walking out the door, she placed her hand above her eyes to block the sun. She looked around but couldn't see Jacob anywhere. As she searched under the sunshine, she noticed the barn door was slightly open, and she smiled; he was waiting in their spot.

She made her way to the hay loft. Jacob's leg bobbed as his eyes bounced around the area. When she popped above the haystacks, a long breath oozed from his lungs as he stood and grasped her hand.

"I was worried you weren't going to come," he said as he led them to a quilt-covered hay bale.

She sat lightly on the edge. "I thought about it, but David was pretty convincing," she started. She watched Jacob's face fall, and she panicked. "Oh, no. Jacob...I was kidding. Shoot."

Jacob stood sharply and paced in front of her. He ran his hand through his hair and tugged at the pieces by the nape of his neck. Charlotte swallowed hard as the butterflies twirled in her stomach. As if her body was mocking her, her stomach roiled, leaving a queasy feeling behind.

His eyes were wild as he stood back in front of her. "Do you think this is easy for me? It used to be so easy to talk to you like you were an extension of me. But after..." His throat bobbed as he swallowed. "After...the other night. It's been awkward as hell. I don't know..."

He turned his head away and resumed pacing. Charlotte sat in silence, unsure of what to say. It was true that it was awkward as hell. They went from talking every chance they got to speaking only when necessary. A word every other moment.

Charlotte knew she needed to do something but didn't know how to fix it. She reached out for Jacob's hand to stop him. He halted just beyond her but didn't turn to meet her gaze.

"Jacob...will you sit...please?" she stuttered. Her hands trembled as he stiffly sat beside her, giving her plenty of room.

She scooted a little closer, and his whole body stiffened. Her heart dropped, and she closed her eyes. Tears pricked at the corners, and she sighed. "I miss you. You're my best friend, and I don't..." Her voice was thick as her emotions overtook her.

Silence pervaded for a few moments before Jacob spoke, "Do you have any feelings for me? I mean...maybe more than..."

Charlotte bit her bottom lip; honesty was her only choice, as she didn't want to lose him. She swallowed hard before whispering, "Yes."

His eyes bore into her. "Really?" She nodded as she bit her lip again. He blinked rapidly, and a small smile formed over his lips. Charlotte grinned. "Wow," he whispered.

Jacob grabbed her hand and rubbed his fingers gently over the knuckles, sending shivers cascading through her body. She leaned her head against his shoulder and sighed as the smell of cedar and lavender permeated her senses. "So, what now?" she asked.

Jacob chuckled lightly before looking her in the eyes. "Just to be clear. You like me, and I like you." Charlotte nodded. "As more than friends, right?" She nodded again. "Good. Then I can do this when I want to."

Jacob leaned down and pressed his lips against hers. The butterflies in her stomach fluttered like a massive kaleidoscope took off. Unsure of her movements, Charlotte mimicked Jacob's movement until he tilted her head and pressed her mouth open. Their tongues tangled briefly before he pressed her down into the hay bale. Nerves sparked, her breath escaping in small puffs.

They continued like this for a while, losing track of time, until a voice in the distance broke through the haze. "Jacob! Charlotte! Dinner Time!"

Jacob pulled back and smiled brightly down at her. "Well, that is one way to stop this."

"Yeah, like when we had cold water poured over us." She chuckled. Jacob joined in before he placed a chaste kiss on her lips.

He grabbed her hand and pulled her up; they made their way down the ladder. He laced his fingers with hers at the bottom, and they strolled into the kitchen, talking like they used to when David whistled. Heat suffused her cheeks, and she turned her head into Jacob's chest. He rubbed her back and kissed her head.

"Bout time, son," David said. She heard loud slaps before Jacob ushered her to the table.

Charlotte avoided David's gaze, focusing on placing food on her plate. When she lifted her head, her brow furrowed. "Where's Paul?"

"He woke up about an hour ago. He didn't feel well, so I gave him soup and put him back to bed."

Charlotte nodded. "I'll check on him before I go to bed."

They dug into their food, leaving little room for conversation. When they were done, Charlotte stood to collect the dishes. She washed the dishes and set them out to dry when she heard static from the radio.

> *Good evening, citizens. The Collective greets all new New York, Boston, and Philadelphia citizens. It offers condolences to the people of New Haven for the terrible virus that has swept through the population. Temporary field hospitals are set up just outside of the city limits. If you find yourself ill, please go to one of the hospitals. To date, 4,525,300,635 people have disappeared worldwide.*

The Collective continues to restore the government and infrastructure...

Static poured from the speaker again, and Charlotte reached for the knob just as a different voice came through.

> *The Collective is evil! Don't listen to them! Their only purpose is to enslave humanity. Fight them! Don't let them take you. I have a message for Princess. The King is coming home. Tell the Queen to be ready. Be on the lookout. Look out for The Watchers. They are the Collective's eyes and ears. And whatever you do, don't go to the field hospitals, they will...*

The original message began again, and David twisted the knob off. Charlotte fell into a chair as her heart pounded in her chest. Princess? She hadn't heard that name in years. Her father had called himself the King, Mom was the Queen, and she was his little princess.

"Are you okay, Charlotte?" Jacob's voice broke through the haze.

She blinked rapidly, trying to figure out what was happening. "I...I think so..."

Jacob placed his hand on her forehead. "She feels a little warm. Maybe she's coming down with something."

"No." She shook his hand off. She didn't feel sick. Just a little woozy. "I'm fine."

Jacob met her eyes. "You sure?"

She attempted to smile. "I'm sure."

Jacob sighed. "Okay. I guess. If you're sure?"

"Jacob," she huffed, "I'm fine, just tired, that's all."

Jacob didn't look convinced, but he went along with it. "Then, you should get to bed." He rose and pulled her up. She wobbled a little before her steadiness returned. His arm went around her as he led her up the stairs.

"Oh, wait. I need to check on Paul," she said as she entered Paul's room.

The blankets were strewn across the bed. Charlotte approached and placed a hand on his forehead. He felt a little warm but nothing horrible. She pulled the blankets back over him, knowing they would be off within minutes. Pressing a kiss against his head, she smiled at his small form before tiptoeing out of the room.

"Is he okay?" Jacob whispered as they moved into her room.

Charlotte smiled. "Yeah. A little warm. But not bad. Hopefully, it's just a bug."

Jacob nodded. "Good." He pulled her into his arms, and she stiffened a little. He furrowed his brows. "Are we okay?"

She relaxed into his embrace. "Yeah. I have a lot on my mind." Jacob raised one eyebrow and tilted his head.

"Are you sure?"

She placed her hand on his cheek. "I promise." As she pushed to her tiptoes, he leaned down and put his lips against hers. He deepened the kiss as he moved her body backward. Her legs hit the bed, and she froze. Her heart quickened in her chest as she pushed away from him. "I'm not..."

Jacob cleared his throat. "Sorry. Not trying to pressure you." He took a step back, and she shivered from the loss.

Her mind swirled with conflicting feelings. "It's okay. I just...I'm not...ready," her voice wavered as she tried to voice her feelings.

Jacob cupped her cheeks. "I know, Charlotte. It's okay. When you're ready, you'll know."

A sigh escaped her as he pulled her into his chest and rubbed his hand down her back. She relaxed into his arms. When he pulled back, he placed a kiss on her lips. "Goodnight, Charlotte."

She smiled back at him. "Goodnight, Jacob."

She sat on the bed as he retreated out of her room. She laid back on her bed and sighed. A smile appeared as she ghosted her finger over her lips. Her mind reeled over everything that happened that day.

Her smile faded as she remembered the radio broadcast. She had so many questions. Was the person talking about her father? She shook her head. It couldn't be him. He had been gone too long to be still alive. The small piece of hope she held onto pulsed brighter in her chest until her brain convinced her that it couldn't be him.

She turned out the lantern and snuggled deeper into the bed. Her eyes drifted closed as the message replayed in her mind. *The King is coming home. Tell the Queen to be ready.* Too bad the Queen would never return.

Chapter 15

"Charwet! Charwet!" Paul's voice rang out into the silent night. Charlotte jumped out of bed and ran to his room. Paul was rocking in his bed, sweat gathering at his brow as she rushed toward him.

Paul jumped into her arms and clung to her as she wiped the sweat with a towel. He shivered against her body as he snuggled deep into her arms. Charlotte placed her hand on his forehead. He was still warm but had no fever.

"What's the matter, Paul?" she asked as she lay down with him on the bed.

"Bad guys took me! Weft me awone!" Paul screamed.

Charlotte shushed him. "Paul, keep your voice down. You'll wake up the house."

"Me don't care! Yew weft me awone!" He jumped from her arms and stomped on the floor.

"Paul. Get back in bed," her voice wavered as a yawn overtook her. She was too tired for this.

He shook his head. "No! Yew weft me awone! Yew no wuv me!"

"Of course, I love you, Paul." She patted the bed beside her. "Come to bed, please."

"NO!" he screamed as he stomped around the room. "NO BED!" He sat on the floor and crossed his arms across his chest. His face scrunched as he glared at Charlotte.

The door swung open, and David stomped into the room. "What's all this racket?"

Tears streamed down Paul's face as he looked between Charlotte and David. "Charwet don't wuv me! She weft me awone!" Paul devolved into tears as he pounded his little fists against the floor.

Charlotte met David's wide eyes as he took in the tantrum. She sighed and placed her head in her hands; the bed dipped as arms wrapped around her shoulder. Cedar permeated her senses, and she relaxed into the embrace. They sat in relative silence as Paul continued his tantrum on the floor.

David was seated next to him. He brought out his puppet and tried to distract Paul, but Paul wasn't having it. He sat up and grabbed the puppet. With a scream, Paul threw the puppet to the other side of the room. Paul returned to his pounding and crying, but it was less fierce. This went on for a while before he pounded one last time. Charlotte sat still for a few more minutes to ensure the storm was over. Once sure, she sat next to Paul and patted her lap. He climbed up into her arms. "I love you, Paul. Always have, always will."

"Wuv yew tew, Charwet," Paul whispered before his eyes closed, his body slumping against her.

She shook her head as Jacob approached. He picked up Paul and placed him on the bed. David saluted and left the room. Charlotte leaned down and kissed Paul's head before retreating to her room.

Jacob placed a kiss against her forehead. "Get some sleep, Charlotte," he said. She stuck her nose into his shirt one last time before she closed the door and promptly fell asleep.

Charlotte strode around the kitchen the following day. Despite waking up in the middle of the night, she was up with the sunrise. She stirred the pot as Jacob shuffled sleepily into the kitchen. "Mornin'," he said as he poured a mug of coffee.

"Mornin'. Breakfast?" Charlotte said as she scooped some oatmeal into a bowl. Jacob nodded. She placed the bowl in front of him before she grabbed her bowl and sat down.

"Where's Dad?" Jacob asked between bites.

Charlotte swallowed. "David was up early and went to the barn."

Jacob nodded as he took a sip. "I'll join him in a little bit."

Charlotte nodded as she dug into her meal. A chair scraped against the wood floor as she took her last bite. Jacob smiled at her and asked, "May I take your dish?"

"Of course," Charlotte said with a smile.

She moved to begin the dishes, and Jacob paused near the window. "Where's Paul?" The room was eerily silent without his constant chatter.

Charlotte shrugged. "I checked on him this morning, but he was still sleeping."

Jacob's brows furrowed. "That's not like him."

"I know, but he had a tough night, so I thought he might want to sleep," she said as she scraped the bowls into the compost bucket.

Jacob nodded beside her as he took one last swig of coffee. He leaned down and quickly kissed her lips, leaving a tingly feeling behind. "I'll see you at lunch."

Charlotte's cheeks heated as she ghosted her fingers over her lips. She stared out the window at his retreating form, shaking her head. Then, she moved on to the dishes, cleaning up quickly from breakfast.

She placed a pot of water on the stove for laundry before going up the stairs. Her mind wandered as she gathered laundry into a basket. She smiled broadly as she thought about Jacob. Despite her worry about their friendship, it didn't seem to have changed much since they admitted how they felt.

She continued into Paul's room. Her mind played like a reel through their journey until she approached Paul's bed. She blinked and noticed his blankets were still wrapped around his little body. She moved over to Paul and recoiled when she felt the heat pouring from his little body. Sweat dotted his forehead.

She rushed downstairs to the well and poured cool water into a bucket. She scooped some hot water into a mug and grabbed some herbs. Running back upstairs, Charlotte grabbed a cloth, soaked it in the water, and placed it across his head. He moaned and shivered from the contact, but Charlotte persisted. The cloth warmed quickly, and she replaced it. This process was repeated multiple times before he woke.

His eyes barely opened—the unfocused, glassy effect reflected in his eyes. Charlotte lifted a glass of water and poured it slowly into his mouth. He carefully swallowed and begged for more. "Slow sips, Buddy," she cooed as she poured another small sip into his mouth.

"Owie!" Paul screamed as he clutched his throat. Big, fat tears leaked down his cheeks.

Charlotte placed the cup down before grabbing a warm tea and honey mug. "Shh. It's okay, sweetie. This will make it feel better," she said as she carefully spooned the birch bark and ginger tea into his mouth.

After several mouthfuls, Paul's eyes began to droop. She helped him lie down and kissed his still-warm forehead. She placed a cool cloth on him as he smuggled into the blankets. His breathing evened, and his body went lax.

Charlotte ran down the stairs and out the door. She swiftly approached the barn, hoping David and Jacob were still there. She opened the door; several horses whinnied as the door slammed against the wall. Jacob stepped out of a stall. "What's wrong?"

"Paul's.... sick..." She huffed as she leaned against the wall, regaining her breath. "Do you have the thermometer?"

David wiped his hands on his pants. "Let's go," he said, stomping out of the barn, leaving Charlotte and Jacob to catch up. His long legs propelled him into the house well before Charlotte could catch up.

As she entered the room, David looked at the thermometer and cursed, "102.1." Charlotte's eyes widened as David stripped the blankets from Paul's limp form. His eyes were open, but he appeared to be staring into nothingness. "We need to strip him and get some cool cloths on his body. Jacob, can you get a new bucket of water?"

Charlotte propelled her body into motion, grabbing a cloth and dunking it into the water. David directed where to put them. They repeated this process for over an hour until David checked his temperature: "100.8"

Charlotte took a sigh of relief and laid her head against the wall. She always hated it when Paul got sick. The first time was eighteen months after his birth. It was the first time she had brought him to the market. Paul ran willy-nilly through the parking lot, chasing the other kids on the playground. He had a blast and didn't want to leave. The joy on his face was enough to give in.

Two days later, Paul was sniffling and sneezing. Then came the cough and fever. It was not easy, but with a few herbal remedies she got from the local healer, Paul got better quickly. That was the worst, but not the last. It had been a couple of years since he had gotten sick and with his adventure, it didn't surprise Charlotte.

David looked at her and said, "We need to keep an eye on him for the next little while. Hopefully, his body will fight it, but we must ensure he doesn't get worse."

"I have some children's Tylenol that I saved from the house. Don't know if it is still good," she said as she cleaned the room.

David nodded. "It's worth a try. But we should save it until it's needed. He's sleeping peacefully for now."

Charlotte nodded as she made her way out of the room. Down the stairs, she prepared some stew for lunch. She jumped as arms encircled her body. She relaxed into their depths as Jacob's scent enveloped her. "He'll be alright," he said reassuringly.

Charlotte swallowed hard. "But what if he isn't? We can't take him to the hospital. We have nothing to pay with, and I can't..." Tears pricked at the corners of her eyes.

"We'll find something," Jacob said as he pressed a kiss against her cheek.

His confidence was of little comfort to Charlotte; worry invaded her mind as she mechanically finished lunch. The three of them sat around the table for lunch. The stew sat like a brick in her stomach. Her worry continued as she checked Paul later. *101.5*. It was going back up.

She banked the stove and did the dishes. While it was warm during the days, the nights could get chilly. David checked on Paul with her in the evening. "102.1 again," he cursed under his breath. "Should probably break out the Tylenol for tonight."

Charlotte nodded as she rushed to the pantry, grabbed the bottle, and winced; it had expired for over a year. She just prayed it would work.

David instructed her to do another cool cloth treatment while the Tylenol worked through Paul's body. Jacob sat beside her, helping her after David disappeared. Snores permeated the silence, and she internally chuckled as Paul snoozed soundly. She checked his temperature one last time. She planned on sleeping next to him for the night.

"How's he doing?" Jacob asked as he removed the last of the cloths.

Charlotte shook her head. "101.5. Not great." The Tylenol doesn't seem to be working well.

"You should get some sleep." Jacob motioned toward the door as he settled beside Paul on the bed.

Charlotte shook her head. "I need to be next to him. He's my responsibility."

"Charlotte. I've got him for now. Go get some sleep," Jacob said as he laid his head against the pillow.

"No, Jacob. I've got him," she whispered as she tried to push him out of the bed.

Jacob wrapped his arms around her and hauled her into the bed beside him. She froze as he pulled a quilt over them. "Well, if you insist, we can both sleep here. Cause I'm not going anywhere."

Charlotte swallowed as Jacob's arms tightened around her. She fidgeted with the quilt until Jacob spoke, "Sleep, Charlotte." She laid her head down on Jacob's chest, inhaling his magical scent as sleep took over.

Chapter 16

"Charwet," Paul groaned as his chest heaved with small, uneven breaths. His pale face shined with sweat in the dim light. Charlotte placed the back of her hand against his forehead and grimaced at the heat pouring off his tiny body.

"Wake up, Jacob," she urged as she tumbled out of the quilt.

Jacob jumped with her movement and wearily blinked the sleep out of his eyes. "What's going on?"

Charlotte grabbed a cool cloth and placed it over Paul's head. Paul shivered upon contact. "He's getting worse," she murmured. A wracking cough exploded from Paul's mouth. Charlotte quickly turned him on his side as he fought for breath. His lips tinged blue with the lack of air.

"Can you get the camphor oil from the bathroom cabinet," she asked Jacob.

Jacob jumped into action and brought the oil into the room. She placed the container beneath Paul's nose, and after several breaths, his breathing evened, and he inhaled its pungent odor. She then rubbed the oil on his back and chest to keep him this way.

Once his breathing was calm, she grabbed the thermometer. 102.5. She showed Jacob the temperature, and he winced. This was not good. "Watch him. I need to get some tea going."

She grabbed some birch bark and catnip and placed them in the boiling water on the stove. Her heart pounded as she stirred the herbs. Paul was sick—very sick.

She perused the various healing oils and herbs she collected over the summer. The stores had dwindled over the winter, and she hadn't collected more this year. Charlotte closed her eyes and hoped it would be enough.

She poured some tea into a mug with cool water. The warmth would soothe Paul's throat, but she didn't want to burn him. She moved back upstairs to hear a heaving cough escape Paul's mouth. Coaxing him into a sitting position, she carefully spooned the liquid into his mouth. Paul swallowed several spoonfuls before another coughing attack wracked his tiny body in tremors.

Charlotte rubbed his back as tears pricked the corner of her eyes. She felt helpless as Paul slumped in an exhausted heap in her arms. She coaxed a few more spoonfuls of liquid into his mouth before he fell into a drained sleep.

Gently leaning him against the propped-up pillows, Charlotte swept his sweaty locks away from his feverish forehead. She placed a gentle kiss and snuggled him for a few moments before covering his shivering body.

David ran into the room moments after Paul fell asleep. "How's he doing?" he asked.

"Not good, David." She shook her head as she bustled around the room. Attempting to keep her mind busy, Charlotte gathered the soaked linens and dishes collected over the last few hours. She descended the stairs and placed the linens to soak as she washed the dishes.

David used the cloths on Paul to cool his body when she returned. Paul's pale face, dotted with sweat, caused fear to surge inside her. David leaned back. "You should try to get some sleep, Charlotte. You too, Jacob. I'll stay with him," he said, dipping the cloth into the water. Charlotte shook her head slightly before David's glare stopped her. "I've got him, girl."

Charlotte's heart pounded hard in her chest as she nodded. She knew David would care for him but was reluctant to leave him. Jacob grabbed her arm and coaxed her out the door and into her room.

She collapsed in an exhausted heap on the bed. Desperate for sleep, she laid her head against the pillows but could not sleep. Her mind whirled with wayward thoughts and worries; the "what ifs" swirled around her thoughts like a whirlpool.

A slight cough escaped Paul's lips, and she bolted upright. She attempted to rise but was pressed back into the bed by an arm. "Sleep. He's in good hands," Jacob said as she laid back.

She closed her eyes and fell into a dream-filled sleep. She wandered through space, watching Paul deteriorate slowly as if life was being pulled from him. A light pulsed in the distance, and she moved toward it. Paul was so still; his small body lay carefully on the blanket. She watched herself as a dream person sobbed against the Afghan; her shoulders shook with each wail. The sight entranced Charlotte before her, and she barely registered her mother's presence. "You didn't keep him safe. You promised, Charlotte." Her head whipped to her mother's voice. "YOU PROMISED!"

Charlotte shot upright. A small yelp escaped her mouth as she fell from the tangled covers around her. Covers? How did a blanket get around her? Her head whipped around as her eyes fell onto Jacob.

She rose carefully, but it was no use. Jacob's eyes popped open. "I'm just going to check on him."

Jacob nodded as he stretched. "I'll join you."

David carefully spooned some oatmeal into Paul's mouth as she entered the room. Paul could barely chew due to his lack of energy. His tongue pushed the spoon from his mouth, and a massive cough exited his body, spraying bits of oatmeal across the blankets.

David quickly patted his back and reached for a bowl of camphor. His breathing evened slightly with each breath, but he struggled to inhale deeply; his small breaths panted as if his body was desperate for air.

"How long has he been like this?" Charlotte asked, almost like she didn't want the answer to her question. She was solely focused on Paul, her body warmed with his singular focus.

David turned to face her momentarily before his gaze returned to Paul. "A few hours. Maybe more," he said. Jacob carefully brushed Paul's hair off his forehead.

"What time is it?" Charlotte asked, peeking through the covered window. The sun sat low on the horizon.

"Around 4," David said as he continued to tend to Paul.

Charlotte stepped back sharply. Four in the afternoon. That meant she had been asleep for almost ten hours. "You let me...why?" Her mouth gaped open as he placed his finger against her lips.

"That doesn't matter. You needed the sleep," David said as he smoothed the blanket that engulfed Paul's tiny form. She stepped back to Paul's side. David shook his head. "His fever isn't getting better. What was it when you last checked?"

"102.5," Charlotte said, placing the cool cloth against his forehead.

"Shoot," he whispered as he stroked Paul's cheek. "It is now 103.1."

Charlotte gasped, and her eyes widened; his fever had gone up. That was not good. "But what can we do? We have tried teas and oils. The Tylenol last night. But I don't..." Her voice trailed off as she tried to wrap her mind around her little boy, who was so desperately ill that home remedies wouldn't work.

"We need to take him into town."

Charlotte swallowed hard. "But I don't. I don't have anything..." she confessed. Medical care was costly, and medicines were scarce in most locations. They would need something precious to trade for Paul's care.

"Charlotte." Jacob shook her slightly. "Breathe, Charlotte." She took a deep breath as the shock of his voice entered her brain. "Don't spiral now," he said. She nodded as she gazed deeply into Jacob's eyes.

David spoke slowly, "That's why you and Jacob need to go to the old house. Glenn left some stuff in a safe in the basement."

She swallowed hard and nodded. That would work.

"Do you have anything?" Jacob asked, his eyes fearful as he glanced between Paul and Charlotte.

Charlotte mentally inventoried her parents' belongings. Her heart pounded at the thought of losing a piece of her parents. Her eyes drifted to Paul, and her body seized. She would do anything for him. Looking back at Jacob, she nodded before moving toward the door.

Jacob quickly saddled Stargazer and placed Charlotte in front of him. He urged the horse into a gallop as they sailed down the road toward her old house.

Charlotte gasped as she took in the rotting form of her house; it had been over a year since she had returned here. Waist-high grass grew in front of the steps. Jacob pulled her down and grabbed her hand.

"We've got this," Jacob said as he gingerly stepped on the front porch. The boards creaked and groaned with each step but somehow held. "Watch your step," Jacob said as he pushed open the front door.

Charlotte's eyes widened as she took in the devastation. A vast hole dripped water onto the rug in the living room, and her feet squished with each step across the room. She gagged as she inhaled the moldy air, whispering, "This... is..."

Jacob nodded. "It's disgusting. But we need to grab the lockbox and bring it back to the house."

Charlotte nodded as she stepped toward the hallway hatch. Tears pricked at the corner of her eyes as her mind whirled with memories of her home. She could almost see her father playing with her in the living room and her mother's laugh as they danced in the kitchen.

She swallowed hard as she pressed on down the stairs. The dust had settled on all the shelves, and small pieces of furniture were scattered around the room, and Charlotte paused. This was where it began, where her life had changed drastically.

Jacob urged her to continue. "Where's the lockbox?" he asked. Charlotte pointed toward the spare room. Her hand trembled violently as memories assaulted her mind. Jacob squeezed her hand and pulled her toward the door.

Placing her hand on the knob, she paused; she hadn't entered this room in four years, ever since that night. A warm body pressed against her back, giving her strength. "You can do this, Charlotte." She looked up and leaned back against Jacob. "I'm here for you."

Nodding, she turned the knob and pushed inside. Stale, cool air greeted her as she stepped into the room. She paused as she gazed around her. It was almost as if she could hear her mother humming as she made the bed. Her hand rested against her burgeoning stomach. Tears sprung in her eyes as she gazed at the bed — the last place her mother had been alive.

"You got this," Jacob said as he squeezed her shoulder. She nodded and took a couple more steps. She could almost smell the metallic scent of blood that had pooled in the bed. Sweat beaded on Charlotte's forehead as she pushed deeper into the room.

After inhaling deeply, she moved quickly to the shelves behind the bed and grasped the strongbox. She heaved the heavy metal and struggled to lift it. A large hand gripped the handle and quickly swung it over her head.

Jacob carefully pulled the box into the main room while Charlotte paused in the doorway, glancing over her shoulder at the room. She smiled as she remembered her mother's smile - the way her eyes crinkled in the corners, her tinkling laughs - all the things she had buried with her mother. While her chest squeezed with the memories, she almost felt lighter, like she wasn't so alone.

Charlotte closed the door, both in reality and in her mind, determined to find something of value that she could trade for medicine. Paul was more important than any piece of jewelry that could be present in the box.

They made their way out of the house and back to her new home. Her heart squeezed as she pulled the key from around her neck. The lock creaked from disuse as it opened with a loud pop. The hinges scraped as she lifted the lid and peered inside.

On the top rested a pile of paperwork stored inside plastic sleeves: her parents' marriage certificate and her birth certificate—all relatively useless documents these days. Births were recorded in local town markets, but certificates were never issued; it was considered a waste of resources.

She placed the paperwork to the side and curled her fingers around her father's medal of honor—his final mission on active duty. She had been six years old at the time and didn't remember much about the ceremony. Her mother stood proudly next to him, clinging to his arm as if she was afraid he would disappear. Now, they were both gone.

She gently rubbed her finger across the metal, remembering his gentle smile and how his eyes would twinkle just before he took her on an adventure. She pushed the medal to the side; that memento stayed with her always.

Her fingers landed on her mother's necklace; the diamonds and sapphires glinted in the lamplight. Intricate metal leaves wrapped around the gemstones, making it seem like a vine. The stones, encased in metal, were made to look like flowers. She smiled as she remembered her mother placing it in her jewelry box. It was one of her mother's most precious possessions. *"Daddy gave this to me as he left for his first deployment,"* Mama said, stroking Charlotte's hair. *"It reminded me that we were always growing, changing and that our love was never ending."*

Charlotte shook her head to clear the memories. Everything in this box had a meaning—a memory, something that tied it to her family. Glancing over at Jacob, she realized that items meant nothing if she lost her brother.

As if a reminder that she needed to hurry, a loud, wracking cough echoed through the house. Deciding, she grabbed the necklace and slammed the box shut.

Jacob jumped with a bang and turned toward her, holding the necklace. A small smile swept across his face as he noticed the necklace in her grasp.

"Okay. Let's get my dad."

They made their way up the stairs to Paul's bedroom. His hacking coughs echoed through the silent house. Charlotte raced to his side as David forcefully patted his back. Yellowish-green mucus poured from his mouth, and Charlotte grabbed his little hand.

Paul's glassy eyes met hers briefly before they rolled into his head. "Paul!" David yelled, laying him flat and placing his ear to his mouth. Charlotte felt his heart beating fiercely in his chest, but there was no movement of his breath. David turned his head to the side and scooped more mucus from his mouth before he began breathing for him.

Charlotte stopped breathing as she watched David give Paul several breaths. A hacking cough escaped his small body before his chest rose and fell stutteringly.

Charlotte released her breath and inhaled deeply as she realized he was breathing again. She looked at David with worried eyes. "We need to get him to the hospital," he said.

Charlotte nodded rapidly as she held her hand against Paul's chest, which rose and fell steadily with his shallow breaths. "What's wrong with him?"

David shook his head. "Not sure. It could be bronchitis. But I think it's pneumonia."

Charlotte swallowed hard. Pneumonia had killed several members of their community over the years. It started like a cold but could rapidly deteriorate as it infected the lungs. Without medical care, Paul could die.

Chapter 17

"Jacob!" David bellowed as he smoothed small circles on Paul's back. Jacob stepped closer to the bed. "Hitch the wagon. We need to go into Ellsworth." Jacob nodded before moving quickly out the door.

Charlotte's chest tightened at the thought of going into the city. Gangs and other groups had looted the city for supplies before the townspeople fought back. When the government took over, they locked it down, allowing outsiders in only for emergencies. Charlotte feared they wouldn't think this was an emergency, but she prayed she was wrong.

"Charlotte. You find something valuable in the house? Something you can barter for medical care?" David asked.

Charlotte nodded as she pulled her mother's necklace from her pocket. David's eyes glistened with tears as he carefully took hold of the necklace; he closed his eyes as his fingers clasped around the item. Tears sprang in the corners of Charlotte's eyes as she released the necklace.

"Hopefully, it will be enough," Charlotte rasped as David quickly wrapped Paul in blankets.

David nodded. "It'll be enough." David lifted Paul into his massive arms and moved quickly to the door. "You comin'?"

Charlotte nodded as she quickly rose and followed David out the back door. Jacob pulled on the harness, tightening the girth beneath the giant workhorses. Salt and Pepper stamped as he finished harnessing them, almost as if they could sense the urgency.

Charlotte and Jacob got into the wagon. David gently placed Paul between them on the bench. "Keep him upright. If he coughs, pitch him forward a little so he can get the gunk out," he advised.

Jacob nodded as he held Paul. Paul's head bobbed with the motion but quickly rested against Charlotte's shoulder. Jacob clasped Charlotte's hand behind Paul's back, gently squeezing as if reminding her he was there.

David whipped the reins, and the horses took off down the road. He turned left and moved swiftly down the road, the trees blurring around them as he urged the horses on through the failing sunlight. The red sky lit the road ahead as the sun began its slow descent toward the horizon—almost like a warning.

After what felt like hours, the scenery began to change. Trees melted into open fields, crumbling buildings littered the landscape, and grass and vines twisted around the wreckage.

In the distance, a large gate loomed across the road, and men stood guard, holding guns across their chests. Charlotte swallowed hard and peered over at Jacob; he squeezed her hand in response as he sat tall in the seat.

David slowed the horses as he approached the gate. A man held his hand up as they pulled to a stop.

"This is a restricted area. Outsiders aren't welcome."

David nodded. "I get that. But my son needs medical care. I think he has pneumonia."

As if on cue, Paul started hacking. Jacob and I pitched him forward as mucus shot out of his mouth onto the floor.

The man winced at the sound. "We just gotta search you. Can't be too careful." He motioned to several soldiers. David jumped out and spread his legs as the men patted him down. They searched the entire wagon before they nodded back at the other man.

"You got somethin' to barter with?" the guard asked. David nodded slowly. "Okay. Royce! Escort these people to the hospital." A man on the top of the gate jumped down.

The guard motioned, and the gate opened. Royce jumped into the wagon with his gun across his chest while David spurred the horse. They slowly made their way through the gate. Charlotte remained silent as Royce directed them to the hospital as if they didn't know where it was.

They pulled up in front of a large building with a red cross prominently displayed at the entrance. Two people ran from the building, one with a gurney and another wearing a white coat. "Flanders radioed ahead that you were coming. What have we got?"

David jumped down and grabbed Paul. "My son, Paul, is four years old. Been coughing for a couple of days. His fever spiked last night around 103 degrees. He stopped breathing just before we made our way here. I was able to get him breathing again, but he just isn't getting better."

"Who do we have here?" the other man with the gurney asked. David pointed to us. "This is my other son, Jacob, and my daughter Charlotte."

The doctor looked up. "They have been around this boy?" David nodded. The doctor motioned for another man. "Get them all into the showers and decontaminated."

Charlotte looked between David and the doctor as they started wheeling Paul into the building. David stepped forward. "Showers? What's going on?"

The doctor paused for a second. "This man will explain, but I need to take care of your boy." David nodded before he turned to the other man.

"Please follow me. I will try to explain as we go." Charlotte followed Jacob and David into a different entrance. The man in strange gear stopped in a white entryway. "Please take your clothes off here. Females this way. Males that way." He motioned to two different doors. "Any valuables can stay with you," he continued, "but your clothes need to go into these bags for disposal." Charlotte's heart raced in her chest. Disposal? Confusion clouded her mind as a female in strange gear exited the room. "Come with me," the woman instructed, pulling Charlotte's arm and leading her toward the door. David and Jacob followed the man into the other room. His eyes bored into Charlotte as he slipped through the door.

The female urged her forward as she stepped into an all-white room. Small spouts littered the room. "Take your clothes off and place them in this bag," she said. Charlotte swallowed hard as she pulled her clothes from her body. She undressed down to her wrap and underwear. "Those too." She motioned to the remaining garments. Charlotte felt her cheeks pink as she unwrapped her body. "Now stand over there on the X."

Warm water shot from the spouts as Charlotte sputtered before she closed her mouth. The woman approached with a bright orange liquid. "Lift your arms," she instructed. Charlotte complied, and the woman scrubbed her with a lather that smelled like oranges but was almost too intense. Her eyes stung from the scent. Inside the suit, the woman frowned. "Sorry about that. I forget that outsiders aren't used to this." Charlotte nodded as the warm water cascaded over her, washing away the suds. "Open your hands," The woman directed. Charlotte held her hands out as the woman poured another liquid into them. "Scrub your hair." The woman watched as Charlotte scraped at her hair. "Tilt your head back." The water poured from above and washed the suds from her hair, leaving it dripping down her back.

"Follow me," she said as they entered a separate room. The walls were white, but blue lights illuminated in rows along them. Put on these glasses and lift your arms to the sides." Charlotte strapped the glasses to her face as the woman left her alone in the room. She stood for several moments, worried she would be left alone. Before long, the lights in the room brightened and pulsed. Charlotte snapped her eyes shut as the room took on an iridescent glow.

She stood like this for several minutes before a soft hand touched her wrist. Startled, she jumped backward, and the woman smiled. She was no longer dressed in a bright orange suit but was wearing pants and a shirt with little ducks on them. She handed Charlotte a set of clothes that seemed like hers. "It's okay. The worst is over," the woman said in a soothing voice, calming Charlotte almost as if she was being lulled into a trance. Quickly, Charlotte pulled the clothes onto her body and pulled the socks over her feet. "Follow me. I will bring you to your father."

At first, Charlotte's heart bloomed with the idea that her father was here, but as they turned the corner, she realized the woman was talking about David. He opened his arms, and she sunk into them. Jacob wrapped his arms around her back, cocooning her in their warmth.

After several minutes of warmth and protection, the man from the entrance motioned for them. "Come with me to the waiting room." David nodded. Jacob grabbed my hand, and we all followed closely behind.

Bright white, windowless walls formed a maze of hallways that all appeared the same. Charlotte tried to keep track amidst the twists and turns but couldn't. The walls had a tunnel vision effect that clouded her eyes.

What surprised Charlotte the most was the electricity: fluorescent lights hung regularly along the hallways, making the white seem even brighter. Charlotte forced her eyes to the floor; her vision swam with floating dots, making it even worse. The man opened a door toward the end of one hallway and ushered them inside. Chairs lined the room's edges with a small window at one end and a door beside the window. "Please have a seat, and I will try to explain," he said. The seats squeaked as David landed his weight against them. He patted the seat beside him, and Charlotte sat between the men. She squished slightly but tried to focus on the man before her.

"So, what is going on? And how do you have electricity?" David immediately asked the man questions.

The man chuckled. "That is the first question most outsiders ask," he said. He shook his head but swallowed more laughter when he saw David's expression. "Sorry. This hospital was equipped with solar panels and windmills before the event. Thankfully, we have several engineers who are knowledgeable about alternative energy."

David nodded. "So, why did we need to go through all that."

"It's just to keep out contamination. It wouldn't help our patients if we allowed contaminated people into the hospital, would it?" The man leaned his head to the side. "You can wait here, but it may be a while."

David nodded as he leaned back in his seat. Jacob pulled Charlotte into his body. She tried to lean against him, but her body was filled with nervous energy. She paced the room while her mind whirled: what if they couldn't help him?

A lead weight sunk into Charlotte's gut, forcing its contents upward. She shot out of her chair and barely reached the wastebasket before the contents spewed. Acid burned her throat as she heaved. Charlotte slid down beside the trashcan with her knees pulled into her chest and buried her head in her arms. Coldness seeped into her veins as she processed until blackness took over.

Chapter 18

A small hand brought her back to reality. The kind smile of the female nurse. "Welcome back, dear." Charlotte blinked rapidly as she tried to remember where she was. Bright Lights. Plastic Chairs. Hospital. Paul!

A blanket slipped off her shoulders as she sat up straight and looked around. Her eyes fell on the nurse again. "Shhh, sweetie. It's okay," she said, rubbing her forearm calmly like her mother used to when she was scared.

"Paul?" Charlotte croaked.

The nurse smiled. "Drink this. It's an electrolyte solution. Don't need you getting dehydrated."

Charlotte nodded. The drink tasted funky but soothed her aching throat, which burned with the fire of a thousand suns. "Paul?"

The nurse patted her arm. "He's stable but still not out of the woods. The doctor would like to speak with you." Charlotte nodded as she looked over at the chairs. Jacob was lying on David's shoulder. Both of their eyes were closed. Calm, deep breaths with the occasional snore punctuated the room's silence.

"That boy didn't want to let you rest even though we told him you needed it." She shook her head with a small smile. "Let's get you up. The doctor should be out soon."

With the nurse's help, Charlotte pulled her weak body off the floor. Her head spun slightly as she stood up. After a few seconds, the nurse led her to chairs beside the boys. Her legs felt like lead weights were holding them down. "I'll get you something to eat. It would be best if you kept your strength up," her perky voice grated against Charlotte's already frayed nerves, but she was raised to be polite. A slight nod sufficed as the nurse smiled and entered the door at the end.

Jacob sat up a few minutes later, frantically searching the room until Charlotte touched his arm. His shoulders immediately relaxed, and he put his arms around her. She almost felt suffocated, but she knew he needed this. His lips rested in her hair as the silence permeated around them.

The door opened, and a man in a white coat stepped out. "Are you Paul's family?"

"I'm Paul's father, David. This is his brother, Jacob, and sister, Charlotte," David said, already awake, as he stood and shook hands with the doctor.

The doctor smiled. "Pleasure to meet you all. Please have a seat, and we can discuss Paul's illness." David sat back down and grabbed Charlotte's hand, squeezing her. "As you know, Paul came to us in serious condition. He was drowning in his mucus. We had to go in and clear his airways." Charlotte gasped, drawing the attention of the doctor. "It's okay. We were able to get him stabilized." His soft smile comforted Charlotte.

"Is he going to be okay?" David asked, his voice soft and calm but gruff as if he were holding back a lot.

"He is stable. Hopefully, he can recover, but we don't know how long. This type of virus can be deadly," the doctor said as he winced.

Charlotte's eyes widened as she swallowed hard; even the hospital didn't know if they could save Paul. Tears gathered in her eyes as she pulled her knees to her chest. She couldn't lose him—the last of her family.

David's eyes bore into the doctor. "So, there's nothing that you can do?"

"Unfortunately, no. Paul is suffering from severe viral pneumonia. His viral load was twice what we usually see, and you are lucky you got him here in time," the doctor said. "But we are doing everything we can for him. It's just a wait-and-see game for now. Our virologists are working on an anti-viral, which will take a few days. He doesn't seem to be responding to typical treatments."

Charlotte's stomach turned over; he was not responding to treatment. Her breath heaved as she took in all this information. Jacob squeezed her shoulder, keeping her in the present.

"Do you know where he would have gotten such an amount?" Jacob asked. His limbs tensed under her fingers.

The doctor shook his head. "It's curious. His body is loaded."

Charlotte's mind wandered through the days, and her eyes widened. "Paul was abducted by the Watchers a week ago." She looked toward David. "We rescued him later that night. Could he have gotten it from there?"

The doctor's eyes widened before he stood sharply. He pressed a button on the wall, and a nurse appeared. "Check Paul over for trackers," he commanded. The nurse's eyes widened before she nodded and swiftly retreated through the door.

"Trackers?" Jacob asked. His brows furrowed, and he pursed his lips.

The doctor nodded. "Yes. Sorry about that. It's possible they loaded him with a virus. I saw it in several larger communities down south before I came here."

"But why would they..." Charlotte questioned before she paused. "Why Paul?"

The doctor shook his head again. "I'm not sure. It seems strange for them to target such a young child. They typically focus their efforts on larger communities."

"Why are they targeting people at all?" Jacob asked.

The doctor stared at him. "Control," he answered. Charlotte's eyes widened. *But what does this have to do with Paul?* "The Collective wants control. If they can command the population, they can remain in power."

"Are people fighting back? I mean...what they are doing...its..." Charlotte stuttered as she thought about their situation.

The doctor shook his head. "Unfortunately, bigger cities depend more on the markets for their food. They need the government for survival. Also, not everyone has the skills. Before the disappearance, most of the population depended on money to buy food and basic supplies. Around here, more people know how to survive off the grid. It makes us less likely to need government intervention."

"We lucked out," David said as he crossed his arms. A smug smile firmly lodged on his face.

The doctor nodded rapidly. "Exactly! That is why this city has been cut off. We do everything off-grid. After the rebellion, the leaders decided to keep to themselves and survive as a smaller community. It makes us less vulnerable to outside influence."

Jacob gritted his teeth. "But it leaves outsiders vulnerable to attack."

The doctor sobered immediately. "I know. But we open our hospital to you when it is needed. Unfortunately, we can't protect everyone."

David placed a hand on Jacob's shoulder. "We know. It isn't easy to make those difficult decisions. But we thank you for your help with Paul."

The doctor smiled awkwardly before the door opened, and a nurse came out. "We found the tracker under his left shoulder blade. It contained a small viral release capsule. We disposed of the tracker and turned the capsule over to the virologists."

"How is Paul doing?" the doctor said.

The nurse smiled. "His condition improved once we removed it."

"That is the best thing we have heard all day," the doctor said as he patted David on the shoulder. "I'm going to check on Paul. It's good news that his condition has improved, but we need to temper our expectations. Paul's immune system is overloaded. It will take time for him to beat this."

Charlotte closed her eyes. While she was glad his condition had improved, she worried it would be too late; Paul was small. "Thank you, doctor," David said as he shook the doctor's hand.

The doctor smiled. "Always."

Chapter 19

Two days passed with relative monotony. They still wouldn't let her back to see Paul, and Charlotte was getting frustrated with the staff. She wanted to see her brother.

She pressed the button for the nurse, and when the woman appeared, Charlotte began, "I want to see Paul. It has been three days since we arrived, and we haven't been able to see him."

The nurse narrowed her gaze. "As I told you before. We are taking care of him..."

"I don't care about that. I want to see my brother!" she yelled. Jacob squeezed her shoulders as she shrugged him off.

The nurse stepped back. "I'll check with the doctor." The door closed in Charlotte's face.

She turned to pace the room like she had done many times over the past two days. She couldn't believe that they were keeping her from her brother.

Jacob stopped her pacing and pulled her into his arms. She wiggled, trying to get free, but he wasn't allowing it this time. "Charlotte," he whispered. "I know you are frustrated. We all are, but we need to let the doctor work."

She pulled back and looked at Jacob's eyes. She could see the concern, but she didn't care. "Are you serious?" She pushed out of his embrace. "Paul is all alone in there, and we are his family. We should be able to see him at least." She threw her hands up and paced to the other side of the room. "I mean, he is four years old, Jacob. This isn't right!"

Jacob slowly approached her. She put her hands up to stop him. "I wasn't arguing with you. I was saying..."

"You were saying that I need to listen to the doctors. But I want to see my brother, Jacob. He needs to know that I haven't abandoned him," she cut in. Her mind lingered on Paul's tantrum from before he got sick. He thought she didn't love him. She couldn't let that happen.

Jacob's shoulders slumped. "Yeah. I get that." He swiped his hand through his hair as she pushed past him. He grabbed her arm and pulled her in for a hug. She stiffened in his grasp. "It's okay, Charlotte." Tears dripped down her cheeks as her mind circled the thought that Paul was alone. She couldn't leave him alone. She relaxed into Jacob's embrace as he rubbed her back. Allowing the tears to fall, she braced her mind against the guilt that niggled inside.

They stood like that for several minutes before they heard the door open behind her. The doctor appeared. "I heard you want to see Paul?"

Charlotte pulled back from Jacob and spun to face the doctor. "Yes! I need to see him."

The doctor rubbed the back of his head. "Okay. One person at a time, and you need to mask up."

Charlotte swallowed hard as she nodded. The doctor motioned her to the door and offered her a mask as he opened it. She placed the mask over her nose, internally cringing at the disinfectant smell that breached her senses.

She followed the doctor into an open room, with nurses bustling around to several patients. A large desk with monitors sat in the middle of the room, the computers pinging with lines dotting every few seconds. The doctor led her to the backside of the desk and said, "Wash your hands and put on this smock." He held the smock out to her as she dried her hands, and she draped it around her body. Standing in the doorway, he turned to her and added, "Just remember, he is hooked up to monitors and has tubes around him."

She nodded as he opened the door. Charlotte gasped as she saw Paul lying in the middle of a large bed; his face was pale, with a tube sticking out of his mouth. His chest moved with the beep of a machine, and tubes cascaded around him as he lay almost motionless. Her chest pounded as she slowly moved into the room.

"He's not breathing on his own?" she asked. Charlotte moved to his side, running her fingers through his straw-colored hair.

The doctor appeared on Paul's other side. "Not now. His body has been through a lot. The virologists just administered a dose of antiviral. We're hoping he will improve soon."

Tears pricked at her eyes as she stared down at his still form. She bit her lip behind the mask, swallowing hard. "When will we know if it worked?" She reached out and stroked Paul's hand.

"We should know if it worked within the next few hours, but he won't be out of the woods yet. His fever spiked last night. He is fighting, but his body is exhausted."

Charlotte nodded as she gripped his hand. "When did the tube happen?"

"We had to intubate him shortly after arrival. He slipped into a coma last night. His fever hit 105.1, and we struggled to bring it down."

Charlotte's eyes widened as tears leaked down her cheeks into her mask. Her heart ached for Paul and his struggle. "Is he going to make it?"

The doctor shook his head. "I am hopeful, but I can't say. This latest antiviral was created based on the virus. It depends on if his body has the strength to overcome everything."

Charlotte's breath grew shorter as she gazed down at her little brother. "I need to leave," she said. She rushed for the door and around the nurses' station. She pulled on the locked door to the waiting room, which banged as she attempted to open it. A nurse approached and beeped her card against the lock.

Charlotte threw the door open and ran for the hallway. Her breaths heaved as she leaned over a trashcan. Her stomach revolted, and she released her breakfast into its depths. Her body continued to heave for several minutes despite being empty. She couldn't believe that she might still lose her brother.

A hand gathered her hair and held it behind her as she trembled. A large hand smoothed against her back. She leaned against the wall as her legs gave up the fight to gravity. Her bottom hit the floor, and she sobbed, releasing her demons into the echoing hallway.

A pair of familiar arms gathered her against them, and she turned into his chest as she wailed. "It's not fair! It's just not fair!"

Jacob sat in silence as he rubbed his hands against her back, allowing her to let go. She whimpered as her stomach turned over several times. A cup of water was thrust into her vision. The doctor stood there; concern laced his eyes as he waited for her to grab the cup. Jacob grabbed the cup and lifted it to her lips. The cool water soothed her fiery throat as she sagged against Jacob.

"I'm sorry," the doctor said as he stood beside her. "That was hard to hear about. I should have been a little more tactful with my information."

Charlotte shook her head lightly. "I would rather have all the information than be left in the dark."

Jacob spoke up. "Care to fill the rest of us in?"

"Of course," the doctor said with a nod. "Can we move to the waiting room?" Jacob pulled Charlotte to her feet. A wave of dizziness swept through her body as she leaned against Jacob for support. "Also, can we get her something to eat?"

Charlotte attempted to stand taller but struggled to walk. Jacob scooped her into his arms and walked her into the waiting room. He plopped her into a chair and gave her a look that dared her to move.

A nurse brought out some vegetable soup and crackers on a tray. Charlotte inhaled the aroma as her stomach growled. Her heaving didn't affect her appetite. Her hand trembled as she scooped the broth into her mouth. It slid down her throat and sat like a lead weight in her stomach. She forced herself to continue despite the discomfort.

When she was done, she noticed the doctor sitting close by. "Feeling better?" he asked. She nodded, and a collective sigh swept through the room.

"Now that she's okay. Tell us about Paul," David demanded as a nurse removed the tray from her lap.

The doctor discussed Paul's condition and revealed information that she had learned earlier. She tuned out the conversation so she wouldn't lose her lunch again.

"Why weren't we informed about this earlier?" David said as he flexed his fists in his lap.

The doctor nodded. "I want to apologize about that. I should have been more forthcoming. Many patients don't have families, and I forgot to update you."

"Yeah, you should have," David growled. "From this point on, I expect regular updates."

"Of course," the doctor said with a nod as he stepped away from them. "I will update you in a few hours when we know if the antiviral was effective."

David gave him a single nod as the doctor escaped behind the locked door. A growl echoed from David as he watched the door snick shut. "Argh!" he exclaimed. He stood suddenly and moved to the wall. His fist slammed into the wall. He screamed as he pulled his fist from the hole. Multiple nurses poured from behind the locked door and stood with their mouths open. The doctor followed them and shooed them back behind the door. "Mr. Woodward. I must urge you to calm yourself."

"Why should I?" David screamed. "You..." He pointed at the doctor. "You kept my son's condition from me!"

The doctor's throat bobbed as Charlotte looked between the two men. David rigidly stood inches from the doctor's nose while Jacob stood and placed his hand on his father's shoulder. David shrugged his hand off before squaring off with the doctor again. "Come on, Dad. Let's take a step back," he urged his father, but he didn't move. Charlotte pulled her knees to her chest and swallowed hard, her eyes refusing to deviate from David's rigid form. "Dad! You're scaring Charlotte!" Jacob yelled.

Like a whip, David's eyes spun toward her, and he deflated when he saw Charlotte curled up in the chair. He swore under his breath. "Charlotte," he whispered gruffly as he shuffled in her direction. He slumped into the chair beside her and pulled her into his large frame. "Sorry, girl," he whispered as he kissed her head.

The doctor approached slowly. "Can I look at your hand? I would be remiss to check you out after everything." David grunted as he held his hand out. He winced as the doctor lightly probed a small cut on his knuckle. "I can't guarantee you haven't fractured anything without an x-ray, but nothing feels out of place," he continued. David grunted again as he pulled his hand back toward his body. "I'll just have a nurse clean the cut and wrap it. Is that okay?" David nodded lightly as he leaned back in the chair.

Jacob took the seat next to Charlotte and linked his fingers with her. As much as she loved David, she needed Jacob right then. She pushed out of David's arms and rested against Jacob's chest. He pressed a kiss into her head, and she relaxed into him. Her eyes felt heavy, and she closed them, allowing oblivion to come for her.

Charlotte woke with a start as a door slammed open. The doctor strode out quickly. "He's awake! Paul's awake!"

They all jumped from their chairs. "Can I see him?" Charlotte asked, looking between all the men.

The doctor furrowed his brows and turned to David. "Would you like to see him first?" David looked between the doctor and Charlotte. Understanding dawned on her, David was Paul's "father." It would look weird if Charlotte went first.

She gave David a slight nod, and he stepped forward. "Of course, lead the way." He gestured for the doctor to lead, and they disappeared through the locked door.

"That was good of you," Jacob said after several moments of silence. "I know how hard it is for you to wait."

Charlotte shrugged as her leg bobbed violently against the floor. "Everyone thinks Paul is David's. So, it would look odd for me to see him first."

"Smart," Jacob whispered as the door opened.

David smiled as he strode out the door and ripped the mask off. "He's askin' for you, Charlotte. Didn't want to keep him waitin.'" David winked at her, and she smiled.

She followed the doctor through the nurses' area and washed her hands. She put on the smock and strode into the room. "Charwet," his raspy voice called out before he winced. She sped to his side and smiled down at Paul.

"Paul." She pulled his head into her chest. "I'm so glad you're okay." She placed several kisses across his head and cheeks.

"Charwet. Stop." He giggled, which was promptly followed by a hacking cough.

The doctor stepped up and helped him sit up. "Probably shouldn't get him too worked up. He's better but not completely well yet." Charlotte winced as she rubbed his back.

"Sorry, baby," she cooed as she helped him sit back. His eyes drooped as he leaned back against the bed.

"Wuv yew. Charwet," he whispered before his body went limp. Charlotte looked up at the doctor, panic shooting out of her eyes as she gripped his shoulder.

The doctor tapped her hand and checked Paul's vitals. "He's okay, Charlotte. Just asleep. We gave him some sleeping medicine a few minutes ago."

Charlotte sighed as she gently kissed Paul's cheek. "I love you too, buddy. See you in a bit."

She walked to the door and looked at her brother's sleeping form. "I can imagine he's very important to you," the doctor said as he escorted her to the door.

"I've been like his mother since he was born. Our mom died in childbirth. So, he doesn't..."

The doctor nodded thoughtfully. "Makes sense."

He opened the door, and she entered Jacob's waiting arms. "How is he?"

She smiled up at him. "He's alive. That's all that matters."

Jacob placed a gentle kiss against her forehead. "That's all that matters," he whispered as she snuggled into his body.

Chapter 20

Charlotte rubbed her arm as she climbed into the wagon. Paul's eyes followed her every movement since he was allowed to see her. She pulled him into her lap, and he settled his small head on her chest. His eyes were a little sunken, but he was otherwise well.

Jacob sat at her side and rubbed Paul's head, a small smile on his face. David shook the doctor's hand one last time. Her heart dropped as she watched David place the necklace in the doctor's hand and a pair of earrings that Charlotte didn't recognize. They must have been Helen's at one point.

The doctor nodded and went back into the hospital. She could never thank him enough for saving Paul. His life was worth everything she owned.

David flicked the reins, and the horses began to move back through the city. They reached the gate and waved to the soldiers as they exited. The sun beat down on them as they made their way down the lake road toward Waltham. The buildings thinned out only to be replaced by trees.

Charlotte snuggled with Paul as she leaned against Jacob. Exhaustion and the swaying of the wagon soothed her into a dreamless sleep as the summer sun beat down on them from above.

The wagon jolted to a stop, and Charlotte woke with a start. The wagon pulled up alongside the house, and Charlotte forced her breathing to return to normal. They were home. Jacob carefully lifted Paul into his arms and jumped down from the wagon. Charlotte followed them into the house and up to Paul's bed. He gently placed him down and covered his sleeping form with his quilt. Charlotte put a kiss on his head before backing out of the room.

"Dad and I have a lot to do today," Jacob said as they walked down the stairs.

Charlotte grimaced as she thought about the animals and harvest, which hadn't been tended for over a week. "I'm sorry..."

Jacob shook his head and pressed his finger to her mouth. "Don't. Nothing is more important than Paul." He pressed a kiss against her lips and strode out of the house.

She grabbed her sewing bag and sat at the table with a mending basket. The strong box sat where they had left it, but the papers caught her eye. She had left them in their plastic sleeve beside the box, but now they were removed and scattered across the table.

Charlotte blinked rapidly, desperately trying to find a logical reason for their escape. But her mind centered on one thing: Someone had been in their home. An uneasy feeling cascaded through her body as she searched for anything else out of place, anything missing, but nothing was touched.

She quickly lifted the strongbox lid, placed the papers back in the box, and locked it. She breathed through her nose slowly, trying to ease her fear. Maybe someone had come to feed the animals and had seen them on the table. Yeah, that was it. That had to be it. She shook her head to clear her mind and returned to her mending.

Chapter 21- Before

Charlotte shuffled slowly into the farmhouse with Paul. Her shoulder ached fiercely as she cradled it tightly against her chest. Although she had been there before, she saw it with new eyes.

She swallowed hard as Jacob set her suitcase next to her in the kitchen. "It's not much. But it's home," he said. Charlotte nodded as she looked around. A large wood-burning stove dominated most of one wall, and a hand-operated pump hung over a sink. "The pump doesn't work yet, but Dad is hopeful to get it working soon. Let's go up to your room so you can get settled." Jacob grabbed her bags and led her up the stairs.

Jacob led her into the spare room and placed her bag on the bed. "There's a dresser for your clothes and a bed. Nothin' fancy," he remarked. He turned around in the room, and she followed his gaze. "Dad, set up the old pack-and-play for Paul until we can get his crib from your house. Might be a coupla days."

Jacob gently lifted Paul from the papoose and held him to Charlotte's face. She placed a gentle kiss against his cheek before he placed him in the playpen. "Make sure he's on his back," Charlotte reminded him, and he nodded.

"Well, Dad and I will get another load from your house. So, if you want to unpack, we'll return soon."

Jacob trotted out of the room, and Charlotte sat on the bed. Time passed while she stared in the distance, unable to settle in truly. She felt like an intruder in a random house.

She was startled out of her trance when a door slammed below her. She checked on Paul and made her way down the stairs slowly. David placed a heavy pan on the stove and poured stew into it. "Venison stew good for you?" he asked as he bustled around the kitchen. Charlotte nodded as she sat down at the table. "Jacob's bringing a lot of your stuff…" She zoned out as he was talking, unable to focus on anything else.

Tears leaked down Charlotte's face. She was now dependent on David and Jacob to keep her safe. Her heart cracked, and her chest opened wide. She pulled her legs up to her chest and let go of everything. Her garden. Her home. Her family. Her life.

Stuffy air surrounded her, and she bolted from her chair, desperate for air. She raced for the back porch, slamming through the door into the cool evening air. "I'll go get her," she heard Jacob say as she ran toward the barn. The only other place she felt at peace was the loft. Horses nickered softly as Charlotte entered and made her way to the ladder. She quickly made her way up and threw herself into the soft hay at the top. The sweet scent surrounded her and soothed her frayed nerves as she allowed her body to release everything.

A pair of arms pulled her into his warm chest as she continued to rage silently. She squirmed to escape, but she was stuck. "Shhh. It's okay. Just let me hold you." She wiggled a little more before conceding to her situation and turned her face into his chest.

His shirt was quickly soaked as she let go. Exorcising her demons, she pounded against his chest as if she could change the entire situation with her fists.

Jacob silently held her, rubbing his hand down her back, allowing her this moment. After what felt like hours, her sobs turned to hiccups, and her tears dried as she tried to wrap her head around everything.

"Is it that bad to live here?" Jacob whispered as if he were afraid of the answer.

Charlotte turned her gritty eyes up to him and shook her head. Her voice rasped as she tried to gather her thoughts. "It's not that. Not really."

"Then what is it?"

She closed her eyes. "It's that. Dad made me promise that I would take care of the family. That *I* would keep us safe. Now, I don't know. But it feels like I failed. I can't keep us safe."

Jacob pulled back. She peeked out from her lids to meet his fiery eyes. "Are you kidding me, Charlotte?" Charlotte winced as he used her full name. "You have done nothing *but* care for yourself and your mother."

"But..." Charlotte interjected.

Jacob shook his head. "No. Charlotte, you have done everything. For the last two months, you have taken on much more than anyone should. *You* have provided for your mother in a way that most adults couldn't, and you did it without complaint. So, if you think for one second that because you need help means you failed. Then you have another thing coming."

Jacob grasped her chin and forced her eyes on him. Charlotte sighed, trying to process his words. She put everyone else first and then felt guilty when she couldn't for one reason or another. "Charlotte, stop thinking for a second. Paul is alive and well. He is healthy and happy because of *you*. Don't ever diminish what you have done."

She slowly nodded. Her mind whirled with everything she had done over the last two months. Her priority was caring for her mother and ensuring she had everything she needed. She never stopped to consider anything less.

A lingering hint of doubt pushed its way into her mind. Her father. He put her in charge, and it wasn't fair. But since when was life fair? She allowed it all to cascade out when she met Jacob's chocolate eyes. "Dad. He put me in charge. He told me to take care of Mom and Paul. I failed when Mom died, but I can't fail Paul."

Jacob leaned his forehead against her. "Do you think your father never leaned on anyone else? In the Army, he was a part of a team. He leaned on people every day. Does that mean he failed?"

She blinked rapidly. Was that what she was doing? Leaning on people. David and Jacob cared about her. Was she too stubborn to realize that? Her eyes widened as she considered it. Jacob smiled widely. "You see it now. Your dad might have put you in charge, but that doesn't mean he wanted you to do it alone. You are a part of our family, Charlotte. You and Paul."

Her chin dipped, and she shook her head. "I never meant to..."

"We know. That's why we didn't push when your mom was alive. But now we need each other. We are stronger together. Together, we will keep each other safe," Jacob reassured.

Charlotte smiled and said, "We will keep each other safe." Jacob pulled her into his arms for a hug. Warmth infused her body as she adjusted her mind to the new normal. The four of them would survive and keep each other safe together.

Chapter 22- After

Charlotte transplanted her peppers in the soil. As she surveyed her garden, she smiled. Over the last few days, she watched Paul improve. His cheeks were pink, and his eyes no longer had a hollow quality. She was no longer afraid to leave his room, afraid that Paul wouldn't be well.

Paul never left the farm, but why would he want to? There was so much for a boy to get into right here. Paul loved helping with the animals. He was calm when they were around, which seemed very different from his normal disposition.

Yesterday, Charlotte freaked out when she couldn't find Paul. She searched the property and almost left to search their old house before she found him curled in the hay. A foal had been born, and Paul decided it would be a good place for a nap. The mare treated him like he was one of her foals. It was frustrating and sweet all at the same time.

He also loved fishing. David's property butted up against Little Webb Pond. While there weren't a lot of fish in the pond, Paul loved to sit and wait.

Life was almost idyllic, which made Charlotte nervous. She was waiting for the other shoe to drop. The Watchers were still out there, threatening her safety, and she didn't think they would give up.

"Charlotte. The garden looks good," David said as he approached.

Charlotte smiled as she looked at the filled rows. "Thanks, David." She pointed to the last rows. "Just a few more plants, and I'm done."

David nodded. "Hopefully, you can get them in this afternoon," he said, putting his arm around her as a smile appeared on his bearded face.

"Charwet!" Paul yelled, and Charlotte turned. Jacob trotted up behind them. Paul sat on his broad shoulders and bounced with each step. A loud squeal peeled out of his mouth as Jacob grabbed Paul's feet and hung him upside down.

"Have you guys seen Paul? He was just here," Jacob said as he swung Paul from side to side, eliciting peals of laughter with each swing.

Paul wiggled dramatically. "Wacob! I am hewe!" A deep belly laugh escaped both David and Charlotte as they watched.

Jacob looked down. "Oh, there you are!" He placed Paul on his feet, where he stumbled momentarily before barreling into Jacob's legs. "Wuv yew, Wacob!"

Jacob smiled brightly. "I love you too, buddy!"

Paul ran over to Charlotte and plowed into her chest. She picked him up and swung him around before settling him on her hip. "Did you have fun with Jacob this morning?"

"Sew much fun, Charwet!" Paul yelled as he went on and on about their morning, feeding the horses, collecting the eggs, and feeding the chickens.

David grabbed Paul from Charlotte. "Hey, little man, you want to go fishing this afternoon?" Paul's eyes widened dramatically as he nodded rapidly. "Well, let's get some lunch, and then we'll head to the pond."

As they walked away, Charlotte relished Paul's little voice telling David about all the fish he wanted to catch.

Jacob put an arm around Charlotte as they watched the pair enter the house. "So, what are we going to do this afternoon?"

Charlotte smiled at the assumption they would spend the afternoon together. "We will plant the rest of my seedlings and then water the whole garden. After that..."

They walked together into the house. Charlotte's heart stuttered when Jacob grabbed her hand on the walk. She leaned her head against his shoulder, and he smiled as they entered the house.

~~~~~~~~~~~~

Charlotte stood looking at her garden with a smile. All the seedlings were in the ground, and they would be great with a bit of work.

"I'll go fill up the watering can," he said as he reached down and trotted away from her. She turned around and felt pride filling her, as she did every early summer. Her plants would help feed them for most of the winter.

A crack startled her, jerking her back to reality, and she whipped around. At first, she thought she would see Jacob, but she saw nothing. Her heart pounded in her chest as a shiver cascaded through her body. "Ja..." A hand clamped over her mouth, smothering any chance of calling out.

"Tut, tut. Ms. Fletcher," a voice whispered behind her as an arm clamped around her body, making it impossible to move. As if on instinct, Charlotte struggled against the man despite the apparent size difference. "Ms. Fletcher, I would suggest you refrain from struggling. I wouldn't want any harm to come to you before it's time."

Charlotte froze. Her limbs chilled from within at the unsaid threat. The man planned on harming her at some point. She swallowed hard.

Her arms were pulled behind her back and bound with rope. Another rope went around her legs, and a cloth entered her mouth. She tried to scream but found making any sound difficult.

"Ms. Fletcher. Do you know how to listen?" Now that she wasn't panicking as much, she recognized the voice. The man from the cave. The Watcher.

She needed to escape. To warn Jacob and keep Paul safe. She didn't know how they knew her last name, but it couldn't be good.

The man dropped her to the ground and began to search her. Unfortunately, he didn't find anything and stepped back.

A few moments later, two men walked around the corner carrying something. Charlotte froze, her eyes widening at the sight of Jacob. She tried to scream again from behind the gag, scrambling toward him only to notice a small trickle of blood on his head. "We found him filling up a watering can," a man said as they dropped him next to Charlotte.

The man smiled. "Excellent. Did you find the boy?"

The other man swallowed hard. Charlotte watched his throat bob with the effort. "Well...umm..."

"Spit it out," the man sneered, his voice growled like a predator.

The man looked away. "No, sir. He's not in the house."

Fire lit the man's eyes as he stared at the other man. "Did you search everywhere!" he yelled. The other men slowly shook their heads. The Watcher's voice remained even, but the coldness seeped into the immediate area, causing Charlotte to shiver. The Watcher grabbed the other by the neck. "Please tell me why you didn't search the area."

When the other man was released, he gasped for air and grabbed at his neck. The man with him stated, "We found that one, and we thought..."

The man sneered before he grabbed a handgun from his waist. Boom. Boom. Two shots rang out. Charlotte pulled her legs into her body and curled into Jacob's limp form. She heard the thump of their bodies on the ground. Feet shuffled around her, but she stayed in the position.

"Does anyone else have any information they would like to share with me?" Silence reverberated around them. "Good. You two, take those bodies to the woods. The rest of you. Get them into the wagon." Charlotte was pulled away from Jacob and struggled to get back to him. A hand pulled her chin to him. "Ms. Fletcher, if you want to see him again, I suggest you stop struggling. His life depends on you at this moment. Do you understand?"

Charlotte nodded rapidly. The gag pulled against her head with the movement, causing her hair to pull. Charlotte winced as she relaxed into the arms of one of the followers. The man lifted her and carried her into the wagon.

They bumped along the road for a few minutes before she was lifted and brought into a house. The moldy scent and squish with each step betrayed their location—her old home.

They stomped down the stairs to the basement. The follower placed her into a chair by the table. Charlotte quickly looked around and watched them dump Jacob onto the bed. The man lit a lantern and put it on the table. He grabbed the gag and looked her in the eye. "I'm going to take this out, but if you scream..." he said, as he pulled out a gun and placed it on the table, "I will shoot your precious man over there."

Charlotte nodded as he pulled the gag from her mouth. She moved her jaw around, trying to release the tension that settled there. "Excellent, Ms. Fletcher." His praise forced a sour feeling into her mouth. She didn't want to be good for this man, but she had no choice.

The man took a seat in front of her and stared into her. Bushy, dark eyebrows punctuated his dark eyes. Black hair fell over his forehead as he pulled his military cap off. "Now, Ms. Fletcher, let's have a chat."

Charlotte bit her lip, trying to restrain her body from screaming. She clenched her teeth and sat up straighter. He might kill her and Jacob, but Paul would survive. That was her only positive in this situation.

The man smirked at her change in appearance. "Hehe. People underestimate you because you are a woman, but the daughter of Glenn Fletcher wouldn't be a submissive wallflower like so many others." Charlotte's eyes widened at the mention of her father. She pulled lightly at her bonds. A little movement gave her a moment of hope. She just needed to keep him talking.

"What do you know about my father?" She tugged at the bindings and felt them give a little.

"Uh, uh, uh, Ms. Fletcher. I get to ask the questions." The man twirled a knife in his fingers. Charlotte swallowed hard. Her eyes focused on the blade as it moved. "When was the last time you saw your father?"

She had no reason to lie about her father. "Four years ago." The man's eyes widened almost imperceptibly. "He left the day of the disappearances," she said.

The man nodded. "And you haven't seen him since then?"

"No."

"No?"

Charlotte shook her head. "No."

The man looked at the other men. "Leave us."

"But boss."

"I said, Leave!" The men scrambled up the stairs, and Charlotte swallowed hard. She kept pulling at the bonds and was making some progress, but not fast enough. "Ms. Fletcher. I believe you about your father. Now, let's talk about your mother."

Charlotte furrowed her brows. "What about my mother? She's dead."

This time, the man's eyes widened. He quickly pulled them under control, but that snap gave Charlotte information. This man knew her family, but she couldn't place him. She tilted her head. "Are you trying to remember me, Charlotte?" Charlotte clenched her jaw. It was stupid to give so much away. He chuckled darkly. "Well, you wouldn't remember me. You were too young the last time I saw you. Around three. Maybe four. But I served with your father. He received a medal for saving me in Afghanistan." Charlotte gulped loudly. "So, you do remember that."

She freed one of her hands as she coughed. "I don't remember you. But I remember the medal ceremony."

"Your father was my commanding officer. He was our leader, and he let me get taken. Extremists held me for four days without food and little water in a basement. Two other men died, but your father. *The Hero*. Saved me and another man." Sarcasm spilled from his lips as he recalled the mission.

Charlotte pulled her other hand free but held onto the rope. She looked over at Jacob. At first, she thought he was still unconscious, but then his eyes blinked a little. He wasn't tied up. She blinked once before turning back to the man. "Do you know that abduction was what changed my life?" He smiled awkwardly. I met the man who would change my future. And soon you will meet him, too."

Charlotte knew that her time was running out. If she didn't make her move soon, she would be taken somewhere else, and Jacob would be left to die. Charlotte grabbed the lantern and smashed it against the man sitting so close. The oil caught fire and spread around his body, engulfing his entire body.

She jumped back and hopped to Jacob as the man bellowed in pain. He ran in small circles, setting some towels and quilts on fire. The fire spread quickly through the room. She reached for the ropes on her ankles, but Jacob pushed her hands away. "There's no time," he said. He swept her up in his arms and grabbed the gun from the table.

The man saw them and moved to block their exit. His words were garbled as the fire ate away at him. Jacob grabbed a chair and pushed the man to the floor. Smoke engulfed Charlotte, and she began to cough as Jacob took off running up the stairs.

Charlotte continued coughing as she tried to inhale the air from above. Her eyes felt scratchy as they made their way out of the house.

Jacob stopped suddenly on the porch, causing her head to bounce off his back. Dizziness overtook her as Jacob pulled up the gun.

"I wouldn't do that, boy," a man yelled behind her. Jacob slowly placed her on her feet and pushed her behind him. His eyes never left the three men in front of them. It was three against one, and they had better weapons.

Charlotte flinched as a loud boom echoed through the valley. She peeked and watched one man's eyes roll into his head and fall to the ground. The others looked around frantically as Jacob crouched over

Charlotte. She buried her head into his shoulder as two more booms reverberated.

Charlotte looked up and saw the men on the ground. She blinked rapidly as she pulled away from Jacob. Blood rushed through her ears as she surveyed the scene: three men with holes in their foreheads, their eyes wide but unseeing as trickles of blood oozed onto the ground.

Jacob urged Charlotte to move, and they descended the driveway. She turned back and saw the first flames lick the house's roof. Jacob pulled her into his arms as they stood, watching the flames engulf the house.

A wagon broke their silence as they watched David and Paul race over the hill. His eyes wide with fear until he saw them standing at the end of the road. "Wha...What happened!?"

He took in the scene and turned Paul into his chest; heat poured over them as the house burned. A laugh escaped Charlotte's chest, drawing the men's eyes. "I didn't think it could burn like that."

The skies opened as if Mother Nature were listening, and rain poured down on them. Sizzling could be heard as the four of them watched the last of the roof collapse into the house.

David turned suddenly and pointed his gun as a figure limped up the road. Broad shoulders, shaggy sandy-colored hair, and a bushy beard, but it was his eyes—Blue like a clear sky. Charlotte choked on a sob. "Daddy?"

The man smiled as he stopped and placed his rifle on the ground. Charlotte released Jacob and took off down the road. "Daddy!" He opened his arms, and Charlotte was engulfed in a hug.

His arms wrapped around her like a present. Tears streamed down her face as she inhaled his scent. "Charlotte. My sweet Charlotte." They rocked for several moments before her father looked up. "David!" He placed Charlotte on the ground with his arm firmly lodged around her. She snuggled into his chest as her father shook David's hand.

"Damn! Glenn. It is good to see you, brother."

Her father let go of her as he wrapped his arms around David. "It's damn good to be home."

Jacob approached with Paul on his shoulders. He pulled Charlotte into him as he watched the men embrace. Paul scrambled to get down from her arms. "Hewo, Daddy! Hewo, Daddy!"

Her father pulled back at the voice, and she saw tears prick in the corners of his eyes. He swallowed hard. "Is this Paul?"

Charlotte smiled brightly. "Daddy, this is your son, Paul."

Her father kneeled as Charlotte put Paul onto the ground. Paul took off and slammed into him. He rocked back on his heels as his arms drew around his son. Tears streamed down his face as Paul continued to chant.

Pulling him up in his arms, her father kissed Paul's cheeks and forehead. "Tickles, Daddy!" Paul giggled loudly as Charlotte settled into Jacob's arms.

After several long moments, her father looked up. Jacob extracted her from his arms and stepped forward. "It's a pleasure to see you, sir." Jacob held his hand out.

"Little Jacob?" her father said with wide eyes. Jacob smiled and nodded. "My god, it has been a while." Her father grasped Jacob's hand and shook it. "All I need is May, and my life will be complete."

Jacob stepped back and put his arms around Charlotte. Her face fell at the mention of her mother. She looked up at Jacob, and he grimaced. Charlotte stepped forward and put her arms around her father. Looking up at his face, she said, "Daddy. Momma...well...she..."

Her father's face fell as David pulled Paul from his arms. "What happened, princess?"

Charlotte swallowed hard against the lump in her throat. "She died giving birth to Paul. I did everything I could to save her. But she lost too much blood, and I..." She choked on a sob as tears cascaded down her cheeks.

Her father's arms fell from her as he stood there, his eyes on the road. Tears rolled down them like torrents of rain pouring onto the pavement. His mouth flopped open and closed until a keening wail echoed through the valley. David ran forward as her father lost control of his body and fell to his knees with a loud thump.

Charlotte ran to Jacob and clung to him as she watched her strong father crumble like the walls of their house. His shoulders quaked with unrestrained agony as he wailed her name into oblivion. His whole world, like this house, was ravaged with fire.

Charlotte turned her head into Jacob's chest, unable to watch this enigmatic man any longer. Jacob bent over for a moment before lifting Paul into his arms.

They stood like that for several minutes before shouts echoed through the air. "Get away from me!" He pushed David back and stood. His fists clenched against his sides. "You promised me you would take care of them!" her father said as he ran his hands through his hair. David stared at her father. "I can't stay here," he said, grabbing his gun from the side of the road and stalking off into the fog.

Charlotte stepped forward. "Dad..."

Jacob held her back before David interrupted her. "Let him go." His voice resigned as he stared down the road that had engulfed her father. "He needs time."

Jacob wrapped his arm around Charlotte as she stood motionless, trying to wrap her mind around the last few minutes. Her father returned after four years only to leave again. Her heart couldn't take much more breaking.

A loud crack interrupted her thoughts. They all looked up and watched as the walls of the house collapsed. The last remnant of her once beautiful home. Her life raft. The four of them clung to each other as they watched the flames devour everything.

Chapter 23

They returned to the farmhouse after the last embers of the fire died. Charlotte was reluctant to leave, convinced that her father wouldn't return if she did. Paul kept asking about their father. His eyes filled with tears when Charlotte told him their father had left.

Despite the late hour, Charlotte heated some stew and a loaf of bread. "Dinners ready," she called as David and Jacob entered the room. A noise at the door startled them as they began their meal. Her father stood in the doorway. Rain dripped off his clothes as he surveyed the scene.

David pulled up a chair and motioned for him to sit. His boots squished with every step. Charlotte grabbed a towel and handed it to him. Her father took it and closed his eyes before he rubbed the towel over his dripping head.

"Why don't you go change," David said as he stared at the table. "You can borrow some of my clothes." Her father nodded as he made his way up the stairs. Each step clanged in Charlotte's chest as she mechanically served dinner.

The three of them sat at the table and ate in silence. Several minutes into the meal, her father stood in the doorway. Charlotte swallowed hard as she rose to get him some food.

As she placed the stew in front of him, a small smile formed across his face. "Thank you," he whispered as he took a large bite of bread.

Tension settled around them as they slowly finished. Jacob collected the bowls and went to the kitchen to do the dishes.

David broke the silence. "Glenn. Why don't you fill us in on everything."

Her father nodded as he took a swallow of water. "When I left..." He shook his head. "I knew something was terribly wrong. I made my way down to Boston before the truth hit me. Cars were off the road, blocking traffic. Half my squad was missing. Airplanes crashed in the fields. It was horrible." Charlotte gripped the table. "That's when I called home. My mission was to help with the chaos. Try to investigate what happened and rebuild if necessary. At first, we thought it was isolated to our area, but as more reports poured in, we realized it was worldwide. That first six months was horrific." He shook his head. "We got some semblance of rebuilding done in New Hampshire before we were informed of a new government. The Collective."

Charlotte swallowed hard. "What is The Collective?" she asked. She knew they had taken over when the world fell apart, but she didn't know exactly what they were. A part of her didn't want to know, that part that wanted to remain ignorant to the rest of the world. But she had experienced The Watchers.

"The Collective is a group of influential people that gathered to help rebuild. At first, they worked as a group, and things seemed to go well. I supported their mission to gather all the people into large places and help feed them. It seemed logical." He wrung his hands. A blank mask settled on his face as he continued, "The Collective formed long ago before the Rapture.

Charlotte's brows furrowed. "The Rapture?" She tilted her head to the side.

Her father nodded. "That's what everyone thinks happened four years ago. All the people disappeared without a trace. Just taken up into the heavens," he said, shaking his head.

"Like the biblical prophecy? The Rapture?" Jacob asked, leaning forward against the table.

Her father nodded. "Yes."

"But that's mythology."

"I'm not saying I believe it. But something made all those people disappear. Unfortunately, I doubt we will ever know the truth," her father said as he rested his elbows on the table.

The Rapture? Charlotte thought it was foolish, but if others wanted to believe it, who was she to tell them otherwise? To redirect the conversation, she said, "You were talking about the Collective."

"Right. The Collective. These wealthy men wanted power, influence, and control. They had their hands throughout the government. Trade in Iraq, oil in Saudi Arabia, and other things in Afghanistan."

Charlotte's eyes widened. *Afghanistan.* Her mind sparked back to the man in the basement. *I met the man who would change my future.* "Are you saying that they were involved in the war in Afghanistan?"

Her father nodded. "Yes. Only they weren't fighting with us. They were fighting against us."

"But that is treason!" David said as he thumped his fist against the table. Cups rattled with the force.

Her father smiled grimly. "I know David. But they were smart about it. They used their money and influence to *help* us. But really, they were giving away our secrets to the enemy."

Jacob's eyes lit up. "Charlotte. Didn't that man in the basement mention Afghanistan?"

Her father's face swung toward her. "What, man?"

"He never gave me his name. You got the Medal of Honor just because you saved him."

"Winston," her father said flatly. "I knew I should have killed him."

"Well, he's dead now," Jacob said as he grasped Charlotte's hand. "Charlotte set him on fire with a lantern."

Her father frowned. "Serves him right. But don't count him out. He is like a cockroach."

They were all silent, digesting everything that her father said. She tipped her head and said, "But I'm still confused. What does The Collective have to do with this now? Aren't they trying to rebuild everything?"

"They portray themselves as this saving grace. Like angels. But really, they are more like a poison, slowly killing everyone."

David tapped his chin with his finger. "So, The Collective is just a bunch of wealthy men taking over, almost like a terrorist cell?"

"Correct, but a more apt description would be like Hitler. They're systematically eliminating anyone who objects to their methods or help."

Jacob sat silent for a moment. "But what does that have to do with us?"

Her father grimaced. "It has to do with me." Charlotte gasped. "As I was saying, at first, I supported The Collective. I thought they were doing good work." He tapped his fingers against the table. "Until two years ago..." His eyes darted around to each of us. Almost like he was afraid, we would judge him.

"It's okay, Daddy. Whatever it is, we understand."

He nodded. "I was called to a small town outside of Manchester called Wilton. The town had been mostly self-sufficient. They had farming and dairy cows. It was a pretty good set-up. When I got to town, almost every man was dying. Some virus had swept through town, leaving most of the women defenseless. We set up field hospitals and tried to help the sick. That was my first encounter with The Watchers."

Charlotte blinked rapidly. She locked eyes with Jacob as her mind flipped through her encounters with The Watchers. "They've been here too," she whispered as her father's head whipped in her direction. "I think the man, Winston, was a Watcher."

Her father nodded. "He was. When the Watchers came into town, I was just on guard duty. My squad was not allowed in the hospital tents, but I overheard them talking one night. They mentioned the anti-virus and laughed like the whole situation was funny. So, I began investigating and discovered that The Collective had genetically engineered a virus that only affected men. The Watchers would swoop in to *save* the town, leaving the townspeople dependent on The Collective for everything."

"What happened? I mean, did they find out?"

Her father smiled. "Eventually, they found out I knew and tried to recruit me. They sent Winston to *talk* with me, but I declined. I walked away from my squad. I couldn't be a part of a government that would harm its citizens to exert control." Charlotte smiled at her father. She knew he was honorable. He grasped her hand. "I met up with a resistance group. They didn't have a name and were quite unorganized, but they were dedicated. I spent the next 18 months helping them disrupt The Collective."

Disappointment surged through Charlotte. She thought he had been fighting, and part of her was proud of his work. But they needed him back here, fighting for their family. "What about your family?" she spat with more venom than she thought possible. "Did we register anywhere on your radar for the last four years?"

"Charlotte!" David bellowed. Her father put a hand against David's chest, keeping him in his seat.

"No, David! He was off helping everyone else while his family was *here*! Barely surviving and wondering when it would be too much!" Charlotte slapped her hands on the table and stood. She stomped off and slammed the door. The small act of defiance felt good after everything they had been through.

Charlotte stomped through the yard on her way to the barn. Soft nickers preceded her entrance as if the horses knew that she needed their calm.

She moved to Stargazer's stall. He stuck his head over the gate and dipped against her shoulder. Tears streaked down her cheeks as guilt infused her body. She had never spoken to her father that way, and while it felt good at that moment, shame plagued her now.

Charlotte stroked Stargazer's muzzle as he lipped her neck like he was kissing her. Her mind wandered to all the time she wished her father was there. The times when things got hard, and she didn't know if they would make it. Anger, happiness, shame, sadness, and guilt swarmed through her body like a hive of bees resting around her heart.

"They always seem to know what we need, don't they." Charlotte jumped and spun to face her father. Tension infused the air as they stared silently at each other. "It's like they can read our minds and give us everything." He reached up and stroked Stargazer's muzzle, who nickered at the strokes. *Traitor.*

Charlotte grabbed a curry comb and entered Stargazer's stall, determined to put some distance between them. The comb rasped against his coat as she moved her hand in a circular motion.

"I thought about you every day," her father said. His hand continued stroking Stargazer's forelocks. "I dreamed of Paul and you. Your mother," his voice choked on the last one. Charlotte peered over at her father's hollow form. Their eyes met momentarily, and she saw a sheen of tears in his eyes. "There wasn't a day that you were not in my thoughts."

Charlotte continued combing, her arm on autopilot. "At first, I was just surviving, hoping you were safe out there. I was constantly asking myself, *what would Daddy do?*" She sighed as her hand fell from the horse's back. "As the years went by, I kept a small amount of hope in my heart that you were okay, but I began to doubt, which was terrifying." Charlotte shuddered as memories swam through her brain.

"I know it isn't much. But I am here now." Her father moved into the stall. He stood next to her, and she leaned against him.

"Yeah. But I needed you then. I was just a little girl, and suddenly, I was alone with an infant. I had no clue what I was doing most days," she whispered. Pain leeched from her body as tears poured down her face. "If it weren't for David and Jacob, we wouldn't have made it."

Her father fisted his hands at his sides. "I'm so sorry. I guess I thought you would be with your mother. You had David and Jacob. But

I never thought..." His head fell. Tears streamed down her face as they stared at each other. "I'm sorry."

Her heart lurched as sobs overtook her body. Her father attempted to hug her, but she shrugged him off, saying, "No." He took a step back as she swiped the tears from her eyes. "You put everyone ahead of your family. You left us when we needed you, and you let me think you were dead," she accused, shaking her head. "I need time, Dad." He rocked back on his heels and clenched his jaw. "Time to wrap my mind around this." Her father nodded. "Time to make sure you're here to stay," she whispered as her father's eyes widened. She wiped her hands on her pants and stepped around her father.

He touched her shoulder, and she turned to face him. "I get you need time, and I will prove it." She nodded as she shrugged his hand off her shoulder. "I want you to know that I love you. Always have and always will, Princess."

Charlotte swallowed hard as her heart cracked in two. While she would always love him, she didn't know how she would trust him again.

Chapter 24

Whispered shouts reached her ears as she entered the house. David and Jacob seemed agitated but went silent when Charlotte entered the kitchen. Jacob stood and approached Charlotte. On quiet feet, she walked into his arms. His scent soothed her frazzled nerves as he kissed her head.

"So, that's how it is?" her father said. Charlotte's eyes widened as Jacob gripped her shoulders tighter.

Jacob nodded. "That's how it is, sir. You got a problem with that?" Fire shot out of her father's eyes, and his fists clenched at his sides. She shrugged out of Jacob's embrace and stepped between them.

"'This isn't the place," she said. "But Dad, you have very little say in my life now." She watched her father's face fall. His body slumped forward, and guilt hit her hard in the gut. She wanted to diffuse the situation, not make things worse with her father.

Jacob placed his hand on Charlotte's back and escorted her to the table. David grabbed the teacups and put one in front of her. She smiled at him as Jacob sat next to her.

Jacob grabbed her hand and squeezed lightly. She turned her smile to Jacob as he winked at her. A shiver cascaded through her body as he stroked her thumb lightly.

"Are we all ready to continue?" David growled.

Her father's head snapped to David, his eyes narrowing. "I get you want to know what's going on, brother, but step back," he said.

David's jaw clenched shut as he nodded as his shoulders slumped forward.

Her father nodded once. "Six months ago, I heard through channels that The Collective was looking for my family."

Charlotte's jaw dropped as she stared at her father. He picked at his fingers, avoiding her gaze as if he hadn't just dropped a bomb. "What?" Jacob said.

"We have some operatives embedded in The Collective and The Watchers. About six months ago, one of the operatives learned that The Collective was looking for my family to have leverage against me. But I knew I needed to return." He sighed. "Travel is hard out there, especially when The Collective wants you. I had to travel from safe house to safe house. Mostly at night, but I steadily made my way back here."

Jacob's eyes widened. "About three months ago, The Watchers showed up at the market in town. We had never seen them before. Heard of them, sure, but suddenly they were here," he said.

"That would have been Winston. He was a low-level agent in The Watchers until he spilled the knowledge of my hometown." Her father shook his head. "He was immediately promoted, and they sent operatives to this area. Winston was their leader." Her father scowled at the thought. "I heard through channels that they had located my house. But I didn't know what they were going to do."

Charlotte swallowed hard. "They kidnapped Paul and took him into the woods." Her father's eyes widened as his jaw clenched. "We rescued him that night. Tracked them through the woods, but the damage was already done."

Her father nodded. "What happened?" His eyes went to the stairs.

"Paul got sick. He almost died," Charlotte's voice rasped as she recounted their ordeal.

"David pretended to be our father and got him to the hospital in Ellsworth. They are still a free area. I had to give up Mom's necklace as payment. But it was a small sacrifice for Paul's life."

Her father grabbed her hand. "I'm so sorry. God!" His other hand went through his hair before he turned to David. "Thank you."

David nodded. "Charlotte and Paul are our family, too."

"I kept moving this way, praying that I would make it before they took you. I saw the flames before I heard anything," her father said as he closed his eyes. His throat bobbed.

Charlotte's eyes widened. "It was you? You took out those men?"

"From the outlook on the top of the hill." He smiled. "I kept looking for Winston. But I couldn't find him, and the flames were getting bigger, so I approached you guys."

They remained silent as if digesting all this news. "So, what do we do next?" David asked.

"I need to find an outpost for the resistance. Figure out the next steps." He looked around the farmhouse. "We should be safe here because Winston didn't know about our connection."

Charlotte's jaw dropped. "You're still going to be a part of this resistance group?"

Her father closed his eyes before facing her. "I have to, Princess." He took a deep breath. "Without me. They are leaderless."

Charlotte's eyes widened. She looked around the room and watched matching expressions on David and Jacob's faces. "Are you telling me that you are the leader of the resistance? That *you* are the reason we were in danger." Her father slowly nodded. She stood and paced around the kitchen. "I can't believe...You...what?" Words failed her as she continued to move. Nervous energy building inside her.

"Princess. I..." her father began before she put her hand up to stop him.

He shut his mouth with a clack of teeth. Her mind whirled around the information. Her father was the leader of the resistance. Everything that had happened was because of him. She shook her head as she turned back to the men. "I can't right now," she said as she walked up the stairs.

Chapter 25

Charlotte watched from the hayloft as her father placed Paul on a horse in front of him. "We'll be back later today after Paul's check-up."

David nodded. "Stay safe. The Watchers might not know where you are, but it won't take them long."

"We'll be safe," he said as he spurred the horse, and it raced the driveway. Charlotte watched as the dust hung in the air behind them.

She hadn't spoken more than a few words to her father in the last week. But he had done what she asked for, given her time. She had watched him love on Paul and was suddenly jealous of her little brother.

He was getting what she wanted—her father's love.

But her mind was stuck on the fact that he had put them in danger. Not purposefully, but danger all the same.

As the resistance leader, they wouldn't stop hunting him. He had made her and Paul a target. Maybe unintentionally, but a target, nonetheless.

Charlotte sighed as the dust settled on the driveway, revealing an empty space. Her heart rattled as she considered her father and brother getting caught. She worried her lip with her fingers as she stared into the distance.

She jumped as the hay bale sagged with the weight of another. "You shouldn't worry so much," Jacob said. He placed his arm around her shoulders and pulled her into his body. "Your Dad is careful."

"It's Paul I'm worried about," she said as she closed her eyes against his chest, allowing the scent of cedar to wash over her.

Jacob shook his head lightly. "Please don't lie to me."

She pulled back and looked into his eyes. "I'm not..." He placed a finger over her lips.

His eyes stared hard into her. "It's okay to be worried about your father. It's natural."

Charlotte swallowed hard. "Why should I? He never worried about us."

"You know that's not true." He tapped her forehead. "Even if you don't want to admit it."

She stiffened in his grasp. "What do you mean?"

Jacob chuckled lightly. "Are you kidding me? You're stubborn, Charlotte. But eventually, you must realize that your father isn't the enemy."

Charlotte pushed to her feet. "I don't think he's the enemy! I think he abandoned his family when we needed him." She stared directly at Jacob as tears pricked her eyes. "I think he put his family in danger and didn't care enough to get us a message."

"Charlotte..."

She put her hand up to stop him. "I can't do this, Jacob."

She walked to the ladder, slipped out of the barn, and went to the garden. As she slipped inside the fence, she fell to the ground, tears cascading down her cheeks. First, her father. Now, Jacob. She couldn't handle everyone being against her.

Needing to do something, she brushed the dirt off her pants as she gazed around the garden. Weeds poked their head from beneath the earth. She kneeled near a particularly dense patch and began pulling up the roots.

"This one is my father. This one is Jacob. This one is the Rapture." Every weed she pulled out of the ground expunged some of the anger in her heart. As she ran out of weeds, she realized that all but two were things out of her control. The Rapture. The Collective. The Watchers. All outside influences. But her father and Jacob. Well, she could do something about them.

Charlotte tossed the weeds into a bucket, brushing the dirt from her hands. Surveying her landscape, she placed her hands on her hips and grinned. At least she had control over one thing—her garden.

She dumped the bucket in the woods as she heard hooves pounding against the pavement. Charlotte whipped around to watch her father gallop into the dooryard. Paul's tinkling laugh echoed as he pulled the horse to a stop. A deeper companion laugh boomed out soon after. "Mowr, Daddy! Mowr!"

Charlotte's whole body deflated. Her knees hit the ground as Paul tore across the dooryard and into her arms. "Charwet! Horsie Wide!"

She chuckled. "Yes. You went on a horse ride. Did you have fun?"

"Sew much fun!" Paul exclaimed as he galloped around the dooryard, telling her all about their trip. A shadow passed over her for a moment. Her father's smiling face gazed down at her when she looked up. She swallowed hard.

"Paul. See David in the barn. You can help him brush our horse." Paul took off for the barn. They watched him jump up and down as he babbled to David about his adventure. Charlotte smiled as David's booming laugh reverberated around them. "Princess?" She turned to face her father. "Can we talk?"

Charlotte sighed but nodded. They walked over to the porch and sat on the swing. "You know when I left here. I was desperate to come back. Your mother was due any day, and you..." He gazed out across the land. "You were growing up so fast. I didn't want to miss any more of your life."

Charlotte swallowed hard. "So, why did you stay?"

Her father closed his eyes and shook his head. "At first, it was my duty. The country was messed up. Chaos was everywhere. Anarchy in the streets, and I wanted to do my part to help us get back to normal." He sighed. "After a while, I couldn't leave. When I joined the resistance, they were so disorganized. Just a bunch of backwater rebels with a dream." He grabbed her hand. "They want to return us to a time when we had freedom and choice without the constant threat of death."

Charlotte looked at the loving expression in her father's eyes. "I get that, Dad. But why didn't you let us know you were alive." She walked over to the railing. "Four years, Dad. At first, I held out hope that you were still alive. But as time wore on. Well, it was impossible." She turned to face him. "You were dead. You had to be. Otherwise, I would have heard from you."

His eyes fell to the floor. "I can't tell you how sorry I am, Princess." He shook his head. "In my effort to do my duty, I failed the people that mean the most to me. You. Your mother. Paul. I will never be able to make it up to you. But if you forgive me, I can prove I'm not going anywhere without you again. I love you, Princess."

Charlotte turned toward the barn. Her eyes filled with tears. She allowed the heartache of the last four years to ooze out of her. Sobs joined her tears as she eviscerated the hollow feeling that used to reside in her chest. Her father pulled her into his chest, holding her as she exorcised the demon that suffocated hope in her soul.

After what felt like hours, Charlotte pulled back and stared at her father. His sandy-blond hair, streaks of gray peeking through, gave him a distinguished look. Blue eyes, filled with love, softened with little crinkles in the corners. Swallowing her pride, Charlotte said, "I love you too, Dad."

Tears streamed down his face as he wrapped his arms around her. "Oh, Princess. Always have and always will."

Chapter 26

Laughter echoed through the house as her father told them all stories about his time away. This nontraditional family meant the world to Charlotte, so she offered seconds to everyone. Paul yawned in his chair, his head drooping from the day.

"I'm going to put him to bed," Charlotte said as she went to scoop him up, but her father stopped her.

"Let me," her father stood. Charlotte swallowed hard but nodded. It was hard to let go. Paul had been her responsibility since he was born. She loved him like he was hers. But he wasn't, and now he had his father back. She should have relished the load off her plate, but it left her feeling lost.

Only a few minutes later, her father returned. "He really does go to sleep quickly." His grin shone from beneath his freshly trimmed beard.

"He always has," Charlotte said. "Ever since he was born."

Silence surrounded them for several moments before David broke it. "I know you went into town for more than Paul's appointment. So, you mind filling us in?"

"I got a message to headquarters. Let them know I was alive. They were glad we're safe." He paused for a moment as if he was considering their words.

"Dad. Just spit it out. I can tell you have more news."

Her father's throat bobbed with effort as he gazed around the room. "They gave me some news. The Collective knows I'm here. Or at least they think I'm here."

"Here, as in this farm? Or here, as in Waltham." David growled.

Her father nodded. "Waltham. They don't know about our connection, but it won't take long. Especially if they come looking for Paul or Charlotte again."

Charlotte closed her eyes and shook her head. "So, that means you have to leave again?"

Her father gripped her hand. "Not without you this time."

"What!" Charlotte and Jacob shouted at the same time. The thought of leaving her home caused chills to skitter down her spine. They had lived comfortably here for many years, and she didn't want to go. But when she thought about what had happened to Paul, both in the woods and the hospital. Could she risk him, Jacob, David, or herself? Was it worth it?

Jacob stood arguing with her father. David interjected a few choice curse words. Their voice rose steadily in volume until she placed her fingers in her mouth and whistled.

Silence permeated the kitchen. All eyes turned to her. "We have to leave," she said. David's mouth dropped open. Her father blinked rapidly, both completely blown away by her words.

It was Jacob who recovered quickly. "Charlotte. You want to leave?"

She threw her hands up in the air. "No! I don't *want* to leave. I said we *have* to leave."

"But why?" Jacob said.

She put her hands on his face and stared him in the eyes. "Because we're not safe here."

"I can keep you safe," he scoffed.

She patted his cheek. "I know you think you can. But none of us can. If they find us, we're sitting ducks here. We have limited weapons and even more limited ammo." She swallowed hard. "I want us to be safe. Maybe that's here. But with The Collective after Dad, I can't..."

Jacob nodded. "You can't lose him again."

Tears pricked her eyes as she nodded. Jacob threw his hands in the air and stomped out of the house. She watched him go as her tears spilled down her cheeks.

Her father stepped forward and pulled her in for a hug. She sobbed against his chest as he rubbed her back. Through her teary eyes, she watched David as he looked around the kitchen.

She pushed back from her father and stepped in front of David. He opened his arms, and she walked into them. "I'm so sorry, David," she whispered as his lips pressed against the crown of her head.

"Oh, girl." He shook his head. "I don't blame you."

"But if it wasn't for me or Dad...."

David interrupted, "I don't blame any of you." He looked over at her father. "You didn't ask for this." He shook his head. "It just hurts to have to leave my home."

Charlotte stood back. "What?"

"Did you think we're not coming with you?"

"But this is your home...you have the farm and..."

"Girl, my farm is never more important than my family." He looked around and sighed. "We're no safer than you. If we stay, they could come for us anyway, and I would never put my son in danger like that."

Charlotte blinked as realization dawned over her. If they left Jacob and David, The Collective might try to use them against her father. They would still be in danger here.

"We all have to go," her father said. "It's the only way to keep us all safe." Charlotte's stomach churned as she looked at the door.

David interjected, "I'll go talk to him."

Charlotte shook her head. "I need to do it."

David nodded before giving her one last kiss on the head. "Go get him, girl."

She walked out of the house and made her way to the barn. Unless he took off, she would find him there. Standing in Stargazer's stall, Jacob ran a curry comb in circles across her sides. "If you're here to talk to me, Dad, don't bother. I don't want to talk."

"Even me?" she asked as she approached the stall. Stargazer put her head down, and Charlotte rubbed her hand over her nose and forelock.

"Even you," Jacob seethed as he forcefully rubbed the comb across Stargazer's back.

"Fair enough," she spoke. "How about you listen then."

Jacob shook his head. "Not really in the mood."

"Are you angry with me?" Charlotte furrowed her brows and blinked rapidly.

He turned toward her, throwing his hands up in the air. "You have to ask that? What gave you a clue?"

Charlotte took a step back and swallowed hard. She had never seen Jacob like this. "But why?"

Jacob's eyes narrowed. "Oh. I don't know—my girlfriend. The woman I want to marry someday just said she was leaving me. So, forgive me if I'm not in the mood to listen."

"You think I'm leaving you?" Tears pricked Charlotte's eyes as she gazed at the man she loved.

Jacob sat down against the wall. "Of course, that's what I think. It's what you said."

Charlotte moved into the stall and sat next to him. Her heart pounded in her chest. "But that's not what I meant," she whispered as she played with a piece of hay.

Jacob's head swung toward her. "Oh. Seemed clear to me."

"Well, if you'd stayed, you would know." She gripped her pants in her hand. "I didn't mean just me, Dad, and Paul. I meant all of us."

Jacob's head swung toward her as his mouth flopped open. "But...we can't...the farm..."

Charlotte grabbed his hands and squeezed them. "What good is a farm if you aren't alive to enjoy it."

Jacob was silent for a few moments. His eyes gazed around the barn, yet he didn't let go of her hands. "Do you think they would come if you left?"

Charlotte nodded. "If they thought you knew where we were. Yes."

Jacob's throat bobbed as his eyes closed. He squeezed her hand as his sad eyes landed on her. "Then, I guess that's it. We must leave."

She leaned her head against her shoulder. "Yeah, we do."

Epilogue

The following two weeks flew by in a blur. David, Jacob, and her father spent hours deciding what to bring. They wanted to move fast but knew they needed things. Charlotte and Paul packed up the clothes and necessities for the wagon.

Paul questioned everything at first, but when her father explained they were all going on an adventure, Paul got on board and began trying to help.

The night before their departure arrived. As Charlotte began to cook dinner, David entered the house. "Girl, I'll take over," he said.

Charlotte wiped her hands on her apron as her brows furrowed. "What do you mean? Don't you guys..."

"The wagon's packed. The saddle packs are ready. All we need is us. But that's not why I am stopping you." Charlotte blinked rapidly as she looked at David expectantly. "Jacob has something special planned for you in the hayloft."

Charlotte smiled broadly. "Well, why didn't you start with that." Her heart pounded in her chest as she removed her apron and wiped her sweaty hands down her skirt.

David patted her shoulder and kissed her head before she walked out the door. She wrung her hands as she sauntered to the barn. The horses whinnied softly as she climbed into the loft.

A small gasp escaped Charlotte as she looked around the hayloft. Old sheets had been placed over the haystacks. Candles illuminated the space. A small table with a meager meal of beans and leftover vegetables from the garden rested on cracked plates. The plates they had thrown out the day before.

"What's all this?" she asked as Jacob tapped his toe.

He gazed around. "One last meal in our special place."

"Our special place?" she said as she looked around the hay loft. Memories of the time she spent here skittered through her mind. In this very spot.

Jacob approached with a smile. "Yes. Our special spot. This loft has been a place of all the good and bad things that have happened to us. We used to play here before everything went to hell, and it was our solitude after." He cupped her cheeks in his hands. "Of all the places on this farm, this is the one I will miss the most."

He lowered his head for a kiss, and tingles and heat spread through Charlotte's body as she looped her arms around his neck, forcing the kiss to deepen. They remained in that embrace for several minutes until Jacob pulled back, placing one last kiss on her lips. His eyes twinkled as he gazed deep into hers. "I love you, Charlotte."

"I love you too, Jacob." She smiled brightly and pulled him to resume their kiss. They got lost in the moment as the crickets sang with the dying light.

"We should probably eat," Jacob said against her lips, almost like he was reluctant to break the spell. Charlotte sighed but nodded as he escorted her to the table. They chatted amiably while they ate their meager meal.

They left the plates on the table as Jacob led them down to the stalls. Stargazer poked her head over the gate, and Charlotte stroked her nose as silence rained over them.

"Charlotte." Her head swung away from Stargazer, taking in Jacob in front of her on one knee. Her hand flew to her mouth as her eyes widened. "I know we're young, but I have loved you for many years. Even before I told you." His voice rasped as he cleared it. Grabbing her hand, he continued, "When I told you I was going to marry you, I meant it. I love you, Charlotte, and I want nothing more than you to be my wife. Will you marry me?" Charlotte blinked rapidly as her heart beat fiercely in her chest. Words escaped her as a smile broke across her face, and she nodded. Jacob chuckled. "I need to hear the words, sweetheart."

She cleared her throat. "Yes," she said, her voice squeaking as she forced the answer out.

A brilliant smile broke across Jacob's face as he pulled her mother's ring from his pocket. The sapphires on either side of the diamond in the middle sparkled in the lantern light. "When I spoke to Dad and your father about marrying you, your father insisted I use your mother's ring. Dad found it in the strong box from your house." He pushed the ring on her finger and kissed it as it nestled against her hand.

Tears gathered in Charlotte's eyes as she gazed down at the ring. Happiness warred with the pain of losing her mother in her heart as she allowed the tears to spill down her cheeks. Suddenly, Jacob stood and pulled her into his arms; his warmth soothed the jagged edges of her heart as tears dripped on his shirt.

As the tears waned, Charlotte pulled away from his chest and stared into Jacob's eyes. "Thank you," she said, swallowing hard and forcing the sadness from her heart. "It means so much..." She choked on her words.

Jacob wiped the tears that continued to leak down her cheeks. "Always, Charlotte."

~~~~~~~~~~

The next morning, Charlotte stood beside Stargazer as she took one last look at the farm—the home she had made over the last few years, the garden she had tended to help them survive the long winters, and the forest that had once been a play area for them. Every nook and cranny held a memory of both her childhood and more. Her heart cracked as she realized that she would be leaving and probably never coming back.

She gazed over to the people gathering in the wagon and on horses and realized that home wasn't a place; it was the people she called family. If they were safe, she would always have a home.

She mounted Stargazer in front of Jacob and sighed. As they moved down the driveway, Charlotte decided to do whatever she could to return to this place and its memories. Someday.

Don't miss out!

Visit the website below and you can sign up to receive emails whenever Hilary Lisee publishes a new book. There's no charge and no obligation.

https://books2read.com/r/B-A-PBNZ-WUSLC

Connecting independent readers to independent writers.

About the Author

Hilary Lisee, author–coffee lover–writes young adult dystopian novels that include destruction, mayhem, and hope. Worlds torn apart by the devastation of war, supernatural events and infection. She is currently working on Tribulation, which is coming on June 15th, 2024. By day, she works as a Special Education Teacher. By night, she writes to her heart's content. She has a bachelor's degree in Secondary Education with a concentration in English and a bachelor's degree in Creative Writing and English. She lives in a small town in rural Maine, where she spends her days around a wood stove with her husband, son, and dog, Sampson.

Read more at https://hilarylisee.com/.